Mornington Crescent

A novel by Kate Blackhurst

Mornington Crescent

First published in Australia by Kate Blackhurst 2019

Copyright © Kate Blackhurst 2019
All Rights Reserved

 A catalogue record for this book is available from the National Library of Australia

ISBN: 978-0-6484867-0-1 (pbk)
ISBN: 978-0-6484867-1-8 (ebk)

Typesetting and design by Publicious Book Publishing
Published in collaboration with Publicious Book Publishing
www.publicious.com.au

All characters and events in this publication are fictitious, any resemblance to real persons, living or dead, or any events past or present are purely coincidental.

No part of this book may be reproduced in any form, by photocopying or by any electronic or mechanical means, including information storage or retrieval systems, without permission in writing from both the copyright owner and the publisher of this book.

For my mother and her sister

'You know full well as I do the value of sisters' affections: There is nothing like it in this world.' – Charlotte Brontë

PART ONE

1

Waterloo

Zone 1: Bakerloo (between Lambeth North and Embankment), Jubilee (between Westminster and Southwark), Northern (between Kensington and Embankment), Waterloo & City Line (leading to Bank). Connections with National Rail and riverboat services. Terminus for Channel Tunnel services.

Nearby attractions: London Aquarium; London Eye; Millennium Bridge.

On June 18th 1815, the Battle of Waterloo ended twenty-five years of warfare and saw the final overthrow of Napoleon Bonaparte as the Duke of Wellington commanded the Anglo-Dutch forces to victory.

The night before, Wellington attended the Duchess of Richmond's Ball in Brussels in order not to panic the citizens by appearing preoccupied with the French attack. When he received news that Napoleon had occupied Charleroi, Wellington deployed his army so quickly that some of the British officers had no time to change from their ball dress.

There was little room for manoeuvres on the battlefield and cavalry from both sides constantly rode over the foot soldiers. Towards the end, everyone was so exhausted that all they could do was stand and glare at each other. It was the bloodiest battle up until that time; one in four soldiers died on the battlefield.

The Millennium Bridge is a steel suspension footbridge that links Bankside with the City of London, connecting the Globe Theatre and Tate Modern on the south side of the River Thames with the City of London School and St Paul's Cathedral on the north. Two days after it was opened in 2000, many people experienced a swaying motion which disturbed them.

The motion is known as positive feedback phenomenon or synchronous lateral excitation. People walking across a bridge will create a natural swaying rhythm and then unconsciously match their steps to this motion and endlessly exacerbate it. The propensity of a suspension bridge to sway when troops march over it is well known, and troops are advised to break their step when crossing such a bridge. Other bridges where this effect is clearly demonstrated include Birmingham NEC Link Bridge, Brooklyn Bridge and the Auckland Harbour Road Bridge.

The Millennium Bridge was closed for almost two years as modifications were made to the 'blade of light' design, and it was considered by some to be an embarrassing failure for the British Millennium Project. Although the bridge no longer resonates in this manner, it is still often referred to as the wobbly bridge.

****

Claire and Jean are sisters. They are also Bramblecombes. Not just any Bramblecombes, but the last of a long line of Bramblecombes. They are expected to marry and renounce their maiden names. There will be no more Bramblecombes. They carry a childish weight of responsibility.

Mornington Crescent

It is Claire's thirteenth birthday. She collects Jean from school and comes home to play with her friend, Elsie. She races up the stairs to tell their mother they are home. Joyce is in her room stabbing at her typewriter, spinning her stories onto the paper like a predatory spider, trapping their essence with staccato strokes.

Claire hesitates at the door. She will not enter and distract the muse; a frequent and demanding house guest. Nothing can interrupt Joyce's artistic seizures, which can last for hours, sometimes days. Claire calls out, 'We're home!' She hears a mumbled reply and dashes back down to the street. They play skipping in the middle of the road. Jean wants to jump and not turn the rope. She doesn't like to share, and Claire usually gives in.

'Teddy bear, teddy bear turn around,
Teddy bear, teddy bear touch the ground.
Teddy bear, teddy bear climb the stairs,
Teddy bear, teddy bear say your prayers.
Teddy bear, teddy bear turn out the light,
Teddy bear, teddy bear say goodnight.
G-O-O-D-N-I-G-H-T.
O-U-T spells out.'

The rope slaps against the cobbles and Jean's red curls bounce wildly in the late afternoon sun. Claire is lost in the rhythm, thinking of her father. He promised he would be here tonight to help celebrate. He teased her that she would no longer be a little girl; instead she will be a young lady. She blushes. She will always be his little girl. She wants to show him off to Elsie. It is wrong to be too proud or to boast, but she is showing off because of someone else, so that is okay. He's the best dad.

Her dad is called Albert and he is a carpenter. His hands are strong and rough and smell of wood and polish. When Claire sings hymns at school she thinks of him 'whose strong hands were skilled at the plane and the lathe'. She confuses Our Father with her father. He helps them make tea and peels potatoes, standing calmly at the sink while they leap about the kitchen, eager to please. He looks down and smiles. Albert reads them bedtime stories. Often he makes them up and pirates, fairies and talking animals crowd into the bedroom.

He takes Claire and Jean to play in the park when Joyce is busy. Once Jean left Lamby behind and Albert took them back to the park at night to look for him. The swings and slide loomed out of the dark with twisted shadows but Claire wasn't afraid. She held his hand and felt safe. Lamby had been put in the shed overnight to keep him warm. Jean cried but Claire was brave. It was an adventure.

Now it is getting late and he is not here.

'He'll be home soon.'

'Yes, and he'll bring a lovely tea and we'll play games and he'll sing to us.'

Elsie has to go home before dark. Claire trudges upstairs, her plaits hang dejectedly.

'Mum, Elsie's gone home and dad's not here yet. Where is he?'

'Hmm? Wait and see.'

Claire and Jean sit at the table, peeling carrots, waiting to see. Claire puts the kettle on. Jean swings her legs and talks to the orange shavings. It is late when the policeman comes to the door and asks, 'Is your mam in?'

Joyce doesn't invite the policeman in. She has nothing to hide from the neighbourhood; her doorstep is scrubbed as clean as theirs.

Claire stands at the foot of the stairs and holds on to Jean who has started to whimper. The policeman looks as though he really would rather come in. He removes his hat and places it carefully under his arm. Apparently Albert was 'regrettably killed in a manufacturing accident at the factory earlier in the afternoon.'

This is not a nice adventure.

2

Embankment

Zone 1: Bakerloo (between Waterloo and Charing Cross); Circle and District (between Westminster and Temple); Northern (between Waterloo and Charing Cross). Connections with National Rail and riverboat services.

Nearby attractions: Cleopatra's Needle; Jubilee Gardens; Royal Festival Hall; The South Bank.

The Victorian Embankment was completed in 1870 under the direction of Joseph Bazalgette as a means of providing London with a modern sewerage system. The project involved building onto the foreshore of The Thames, narrowing the river, and demolishing much expensive riverside property. Tunnels for the District Line were built under the Embankment and on the surface there were new roads, elaborate gardens and many statues.

Travel guides now refer to it as a place for lovers to stroll along the riverside or sit on one of the many wrought iron park benches.

The nearby Cleopatra's Needle is an obelisk which has nothing to do with Cleopatra, although it did originally come from Egypt. It was a present from the ruler of Egypt and Sudan in recognition of British victories at the Battles of the Nile and Alexandria in 1801. Britain accepted the gift but wouldn't pay for its transportation – it was very heavy. The monument remained in Alexandria until 1877 when it was shipped to London via a shipwreck in the Bay of Biscay, rescue by a Glasgow steamer, and repairs at Ferrol in Spain.

****

Claire is dying. She understands that she might have a broken heart, but the blood is seeping from between her legs and she doesn't know how to make it stop. She feels faint and voices fade in and out. There are people and sandwiches and the smell of sweet sherry, which makes her feel sick. Her dad could help but her dad is dead. That's why they're here. She has to remember to look after Jean whose little face is so ashen even the freckles have paled.

'Ashes to ashes, dust to dust.'

Claire tastes the dust on her tongue. Her mouth is dry and her head hurts. Perhaps it's from the singing. She sang at the funeral in the church, lifting her voice to the heavens as she had been taught. Although she didn't feel like praising anything, there was comfort in the ritual. People came together and paid their respects. Men stood twisting their caps and Albert's friends sang lustily which didn't seem out of place in the sombre church. Aunty Beatrice seemed out of place, there as now, wearing a tight fitting black carapace.

Joyce is in the front room, shaking hands and looking bemused. Her hair escapes from the pin that clasps it, as she longs to escape from the muffled voices and sincere condolences. Claire pours more tea and looks down into the swirling cups. She is aware of Aunty Beatrice, inspecting the china and prospecting for dust. Claire knows there won't be any. She has scoured this house, wiping away all traces. But her body is letting her down and she feels so ashamed. And scared.

Gordon sits Jean on his lap and plays shadow puppets until her whimpers subside. Gordon is her dad's best friend. Should that be was? Gordon still is, even if Albert isn't. The thought makes a tear splash into a saucer and Claire squeezes her eyes shut and rocks. She thinks of Alice in Wonderland and all those tears she cried, until she created a deep pool that she fell into, and nearly drowned. There was a rhyme Alice recited to see if she had reason. Claire tries it:

'How doth the little crocodile improve his shining tail,
And pour the waters of the Nile on every golden scale!
How cheerfully he seems to grin, how neatly spread his claws,
And welcome little fishes in with gently smiling jaws!'

It doesn't work. She hears a strangled noise and turns to see Aunty Beatrice. She almost smiles as she wonders absently whether she might be one of the curious creatures that fell in the pool, but Aunty Beatrice's expression suggests this is no place for amusement. She has been clearing her throat preparatory to making a speech.

'You may be young, but you have to learn to be tough in times like these. You'll be grieving for your father, as we all are, God rest his soul. But you must know that your mother needs help.'

Claire glances towards Joyce, swaying slightly, a lone monument in the centre of the room, lost in her thoughts. She doesn't look like she needs help; she looks quite happy. She must be thinking of Albert because the sweetest smile rests on her face. Claire knows that the Bramblecombe family don't approve. She has heard words like 'flighty' and 'disreputable' linked with 'lady novelist' and raised eyebrows accompanied by pursed lips. The relatives have been noticeable for their absence, for many of them today is their first visit to this house and they sit with their coats clutched about them, fearful of catching some unspeakable disease; creativity or imagination perhaps.

'You're a part of the family, and we want to do right by you and your sister. You can stay with one of us and someone from the hospital can look after your mother.'

Aunty Beatrice falters. There is something cold in the way Claire is looking at her; a fierce determination that has no place in a young girl, but actually looks a lot like Albert when he got one of his foolish notions. Such as marrying an artistic type who was weak in the head and spent half her days behind closed doors scribbling God knows what. Claire shakes her head, her lips are moving soundlessly. Aunty Beatrice tries again.

'We only want to help, and your mother can't take care of you. You are the eldest and must start making some sensible decisions. Come and join our family or...'

The threat hangs in the air like a malignant balloon. Claire punctures it with semantic needles.

'We're staying here. You get out of our house.'

She is shaking as she runs up the stairs and throws herself onto the bed, crying once again, even though she thought she was dried up. Blood flows out of her with the tears and her life. When she feels a cool hand on her forehead and someone tucks her into her bed, she can't be sure if it's the duchess, the white rabbit, the queen of hearts, or her mother.

3

Temple

Zone 1: Circle and District (between Embankment and Blackfriars).

Nearby attractions: Hayward Gallery; Somerset House; Temple and Middle Temple.

The Knights Templar were a chivalrous order founded in 1118 to protect pilgrims on their way to the Holy Land. The order owned land in the centre of London until 1312 when it was confiscated by the Crown on the grounds of immorality and heresy, but in reality the order had become wealthy and was a threat to the throne.

The Middle Temple and the Inner Temple represent two of London's four Inns of Court, along with Gray's Inn and Lincoln's Inn. The four inns fulfil the same function, but each has its separate traditions. According to ancient custom, any law student training to be a barrister in Britain must join one of the Inns of Court and dine there twenty-four times, as well as passing their exams, before being officially qualified.

Temple Bar is the gateway marking the westward limit of the City of London.

Somerset House is a centre for arts and culture in the heart of London, with 55 dancing fountains which make way for an open-air ice-rink in winter. The building began as a palace built by Edward Seymour. He was the uncle of Edward VI, who was too young to rule when his father, Henry VIII died in 1547. Seymour became Lord Protector and Duke of Somerset and built himself a residence befitting his new rank, clearing a site between the Thames and the Strand, and demolishing several churches and chapels in the process.

The Privy Council were not best pleased by this development and it led to Somerset's arrest and brief imprisonment in the Tower of London in 1549. Two years later he was arrested again, this time for treason, and executed on Tower Hill.

****

The 'Compensation' is no recompense. Joyce shuts herself away and devotes herself to her work. No longer a labour of love, she struggles with every word. Claire has seen her red eyes and wonders if tears weave their way into her tales; whether her stories have become full of bitterness, sorrow and recriminations. The girls have never seen their mother's work, although they know she has meetings with her editor and her publisher. Perhaps she writes under a pseudonym? Perhaps she writes racy tales of murder and seduction? Claire smiles to think of such things being concocted under her roof.

Claire looks after Jean and cleans the house with little complaint. Although it isn't fair, she is terrified that Aunty Beatrice will come back and take them away. She knows their situation may not be 'normal' but she clings to it. It is what she knows and who wants to be normal anyway? Normal is dull; ordinary; average; middling; common; typical; lacklustre; boring; tedious; monotonous; dreary (she has been reading her thesaurus). Normal is school uniforms worn correctly; shepherd's pie without carrots and peas; not voicing your opinion in case you get laughed at; aspiring to work in the factory or even be a secretary.

Claire and Elsie have a club, full of rules and secrets and codes. One of the codes involves the patterns of dots on dice. It is so brilliant that they can't remember it from week to week so it is constantly evolving. They hold roll calls (even though there are just the two of them) and have special handshakes and passwords. The club has several different sub-sects including one where they make up routines to Fred Astaire and Cole Porter songs and lip-synch the words into their hairbrushes. 'A Fine Romance' is one of their favourites, although they fight over who gets to be Ginger.

Without Elsie, Claire plays with her kitten, which she rescued from the river. It is a small grey thing with a white paw which had been left to its fate. In this case, its fate was a group of boys with pointy faces and sharp rocks upon whom Claire swept down like an avenging angel. They ran from her wrath and left the poor kitten cut, bruised and blind in one eye. Of course Claire took her home and though Joyce didn't like cats or want another mouth to feed, she could hardly deny her daughter's Samaritan spirit and so allowed Grimalkin to stay. Now Grimalkin is a cowardly cat who runs to greet Claire with tail aloft when she gets home from school but hides from everyone else apart from the neighbourhood dogs which she attacks with spitting ferocity.

Religion also comforts Claire. She likes the rhymes and the rituals, the stories and the sacraments. She dislikes the omnipotent (and, quite frankly, nosey) God and prefers His son with His meek manner and artisan origins. She loves singing hymns and reciting prayers, although she doesn't know what she believes. When she receives the benediction and is told to 'Go with God' she wonders, where? Sometimes she wishes she were a Catholic so she could sit in the confessional and have a private audience. She does not want to be absolved, but she does want to be heard; to have the luxury of someone listening to her and only her.

Her favourite story is The Resurrection. Although she knows that death is final, she cherishes a dream that she does not divulge; that one day her father will come back for her.

'I am the Resurrection and the life: he that believeth in me, though he were dead, yet shall he live: And whosoever liveth and believeth in me shall never die.'

This is one of the stories she tells Jean before she falls asleep and Jean dreams of sheep wandering blissfully through green pastures as she floats above still waters with arms outstretched.

Although she is not a religious woman, Joyce smiles at Claire's enthusiasm and likes the idea of an Easter Festival. She buys two small Easter eggs and places them at their bedsides so they will see them in the morning. Claire is overwhelmed by the gesture. Jean is simply overwhelmed by the chocolate and she devours her egg immediately. Sidling up to her sister, she is shocked when

Claire guards her egg jealousy. Claire has never withheld anything from her before.

When Claire is playing outside with Elsie, Jean covets Claire's egg. Claire has made no attempt to conceal it. If she didn't want Jean to have it, surely she would have hidden it from her? Jean unwraps the shiny paper and breathes in the heady aroma. She has to feel the silky decadence in her mouth. She breaks off a little bit and savours its sweetness on her tongue. Wrapping up the egg with a chunk missing is quite difficult, but it looks plausible from the outside. Claire doesn't notice anything amiss when she comes home that night. She doesn't notice the next night either or the next as Jean consumes the glossy, sugary chocolate bit by delicious bit.

Plagued by belated guilt, Jean configures the paper into an oval shape and puts it back. Perhaps Claire doesn't want to eat it; perhaps she only wants to look at it. As the days pass and Claire shows no sign of starting on her egg, Jean forgets all about it. When Claire discovers her gleaming gift is not only hollow, but empty she is bitterly disappointed. She loves Jean very much, but honestly!

4

Tower Hill

Zone 1: Circle (between Monument and Aldgate); District (between Monument and Aldgate East). Connections with National Rail and riverboat services.

Nearby attractions: Tower Bridge; Tower of London; Tower Hill Memorial.

Archaeological evidence shows that there was a settlement on Tower Hill during the Bronze Age. Later there was a Roman village which was burnt down during the Boadicea uprising. Now there remains one of the largest segments of the Roman wall that formerly surrounded the City of London. Public executions of high-profile criminals were conducted on the hill.

The nearby Tower of London is officially Her Majesty's Palace and Fortress, although the last royal resident was King James I (1566-1625). A royal menagerie was established at the Tower in the thirteenth century when Henry III received a wedding gift of three leopards. Home to lions and tigers, it was here that William Blake saw the tiger that inspired his poem. It was occasionally opened to the public by Elizabeth I, but the big cats were woefully neglected and the collection was closed in 1835 when the last of the animals were moved to London Zoo.

The Tower Hill Memorial is a national war memorial which commemorates those from the Merchant Navy and fishing fleets who died during both world wars and have no known grave.

****

Bonfire night! The words are magical, and Jean and Claire are full of excitement. Joyce is taking them to see a display at the local park. It is a rare outing with their mother and they each cling to a hand, as if she is some will-o-the-wisp who might be called away by the drifting smoke if they don't hold on tight.

It is a crisp evening and they are wrapped up in coats and mittens. Joyce wears a fur around her neck, which Jean strokes with admiration. The air smells of wood smoke, and shouts and laughter ring up and down the streets. As they march along the avenue, Jean skips and scuffs through the fallen leaves. She chants as she prances:

'Remember, remember the fifth of November
Gunpowder treason and plot,
We see no reason
Why gunpowder treason
Should ever be forgot.'

She has learned this at school and her class has been 'doing Guy Fawkes'. They have written poems and drawn pictures which adorn the walls of their classroom. Jean's contribution is a collage. She has cut up scraps of material and images from magazines in bright scarlet, crimson, ruby, vermillion, orange, gold and burnished burgundy, overlapping them to make licking and leaping flames. They have also made treacle toffee, which Jean proudly brought home and they all glued their gums together, sitting in the kitchen snorting and pulling facial contortions as they tried to open their mouths.

Claire has always wondered whether they are celebrating the fact that Guy Fawkes tried to blow up The Houses of Parliament, or the fact that he failed. A trio of boys wheel past with an effigy in a barrow. 'Penny for the guy' they ask hopefully. Joyce stops them and inspects their mannequin. His head is a football with straw on top and he is dressed in an old tweed suit with stalks sticking out of his sleeves and creeping over the top button of his waistcoat like a particularly hirsute scarecrow. She unclasps her purse and gives them a coin for their trouble and they whistle off down the street.

Ahead they see torches beckoning the procession to the bonfire in the centre of the park. There is a roaring in the air as the bearers brandish their flaming wands and their faces are lit with a strangely demonic glow. The pile of sticks and leaves is illuminated – it is a big one. Claire has seen the gangs of boys protecting their individual bonfires around town. As soon as they are called in for supper, some hooligan nicks their kindling and fights break out. Claire wades into their circle and checks that there are no hedgehogs hidden in their flammable mountains. The boys allow her to pass among them like an untouchable Francis of Assisi.

Later, as they stand around the embers, they hold hot potatoes in tin foil which have been baked in the huge conflagration. Jean and Claire toss them from mitten to mitten as they are still too hot to handle. They have lumps of parkin in their pockets and look forward to the tingling ginger taste mixed with oatmeal and syrup. Fireworks explode above: rockets and bangs; sparks and stars; fizzes and squeals. Roman candles and dragons eggs.

Claire likes the fountains in their hails of green, pink and gold. Jean waves a sparkler inscribing her name against black with gilt filigree. They watch the Catherine Wheel pinned to a post as it whirls and crackles spitting out tongues of dazzling fire. Claire knows it is named after an instrument of torture, and she thinks to herself, 'How cruel we are'.

When they arrive home, they are tired and ready for bed. Claire calls for Grimalkin, but he doesn't come running. She hopes he isn't too scared by all the lights and noise. She heats the milk in a pan on the stove and pours it into two mugs. Joyce has a tot of whisky and they sit in the kitchen in silence. Jean's head slumps forward and her eyelids flicker as she mumbles about never forgetting. Claire smiles and, wiping the milk from her upper lip, she half carries half drags Jean up to bed. As she lies between the cool sheets, listening to Jean babble in her sleep, she leaves the curtains open to see the sky erupting overhead like a fantastic volcano.

****

The next morning, Claire finds a cold damp heap curled foetus-like on the doorstep. She can barely recognise Grimalkin with a spent firework tied to his tail.

5

Whitechapel

Zone 2: District and Hammersmith & City (between Aldgate East and Stepney Green), East London (between Shadwell and Shoreditch).

Nearby attractions: Albion Brewery & Blind Beggar Pub; Freedom Press; Whitechapel Art Gallery.

Extreme poverty, homelessness, exploitative work conditions, prostitution and infant mortality in the area alongside great personal wealth, made Whitechapel a fertile ground for reformers and revolutionaries. In Whitechapel George Bernard Shaw's Fabian Society met regularly, Vladimir Ilyich Lenin led rallies, William Booth established the Salvation Army, and Charlotte Wilson founded the Freedom Press which remains as the oldest surviving anarchist publishing house in the English speaking world.

The Whitechapel Murderer of 1888 later became known as Jack the Ripper, whose gory exploits became the salacious fodder for burgeoning newspapers. The identity of the killer has never been confirmed, leading to a plethora of conspiracy theories, legends and dubious amateur sleuthing. In 2006 Jack the Ripper was selected by the readers of the BBC History Magazine as 'the worst Briton in history'.

The bloody thread continues through the district as the gangland mobs of the 1960s frequented the area. In 1966 Ronnie Kray (of the notorious Kray twins) shot and killed one of his rivals in the Blind Beggar Pub, which is popular with tourists looking for a vicarious thrill from these sinister days of London.

****

It is school sports day. The children line up and run and jump and throw things, all aiming to be the best; to run the fastest, jump the highest, throw the farthest. The teachers hand out drinks of lemon squash and hold pieces of tape to measure distances. The mothers stand around under white hats in the sun and laugh. They encourage occasionally, but mainly they gossip, sizing up each other's children looking for reflections of imagined faults.

Jean is competing at long jump. She races up to the white board and flings herself dramatically into the sandpit, trying to make her legs overtake her body. She shakes the sand out of her baggy britches. Part of the school uniform is this PE kit which consists of a pale blue cotton vest and big navy blue bloomers. The giggling girls call them 'harvest festivals' because 'all is safely gathered in'.

Claire stands by to cheer on Jean's efforts. She is pleased they are in the same house. There are Brontë, Hardy, Dickens and Elliot. They are in Brontë which is blue. Elsie is in Dickens which is yellow. Hardy are red and always win everything. Claire hates having to compete against Elsie. In the running race, she stops and waits for her, so that they can cross the line together holding hands, even though Claire is clearly out in front.

When Jean wins the long jump for the middle school, Claire is thrilled. There is a presentation for the winners at the end of the day and they must all file up onto a podium and shake hands with Miss Higgins, the deputy head mistress. Claire sits on the stage with the other prefects and she sees Jean grinning up at her, waiting for her big moment. Claire gives a supportive smile, although she cringes inside at Jean's appearance. The school uniform also necessitates a beret which, try as she might, will never sit primly on Jean's curls but springs off at a rakish angle. It seems to annoy Miss Higgins intensely, as though its disobedient behaviour is a personal affront. She frequently remonstrates with Jean whose height and red hair single her out from the crowd, even if her big smile and eager enthusiasm don't.

'First in long jump, Miss Bramblecombe.'

Miss Higgins turns to Claire, expecting her to come forward. Claire shakes her head and nods towards the steps where Jean is stumbling forward. She sees Miss Higgins frown imperceptibly.

'Oh, that Miss Bramblecombe. Well, it's heartening to see that you're good at something at least.'

A small snigger runs around the hall and Jean blushes. She trips and sprawls across the stage, her beret flying from her head and for once landing neatly at Miss Higgins' feet. The titter increases and Miss Higgins smiles a tight smile. Claire looks at the mothers and their children standing smugly in the hall and enjoying Jean's discomfort. Jean gets to her feet and throws a bemused glance at Claire; she thought she had done something right, why is this going wrong? Claire nods and smiles fiercely at her. Miss Higgins voice drips acid.

'There's no need to show off your winning style now.'

To more peals of laughter Miss Higgins pushes the beret across the stage so that Jean has to stoop to pick it up. She holds out the certificate between finger and thumb.

'What a pity that your poor mother couldn't be here to witness your triumph. But then, I don't suppose she thinks it's very important.'

Tears fill Jean's eyes as Claire springs to her feet and strides towards her. She puts her arm around her and glares at Miss Higgins, snatching the certificate from her.

'That's enough' she hisses. 'You made my sister cry, you nasty woman.'

Miss Higgins is taken aback. Perhaps she went too far.

'There, now, don't get upset, I was only joking.'

'Jokes are meant to be funny.'

Claire escorts Jean from the stage and leaves school early. She raids her piggy-bank and buys a wooden frame for Jean's certificate of achievement.

****

Claire is very good at sports. She is also good at schoolwork. She excels at maths because she is forced to budget at home and learned how many sausages she could get with change from a designated amount of shillings long before they were ever taught arithmetic in class. If asked, she could also say where to get the best and the cheapest – not always the same thing – produce from around town. She is never asked.

Her favourite topics are English and History. She loves to learn about other worlds, making friends with characters in the pages of books. Jean doesn't catch the reading bug and prefers to hear the stories that Claire reads aloud. Her favourites are *The Adventures of the Wishing Chair* and *The Faraway Tree*. She loves the thrilling escapades of the children with their sensible names who are always home in time for tea. When they run out, she clamours for more and Claire invents more magical lands and adventures for Moon Face.

Claire takes Jean to the library and leaves her to explore her own imaginary worlds. She is allowed four books at a time and has a system for choosing her reading material. First of all, she wanders awestruck along the aisles. She is overwhelmed by all those hidden words making all those sentences, chapters and stories, pressed tightly between pages like precious flowers. She always hopes to find her mother's name emblazoned on a leather spine, but she never does.

She chooses a book that is educational. It may tell her about ancient Greece or how children live in African tribes. She likes stories of endeavour and has read all about the building of the pyramids and the invention of the steam engine. The second is by an author that she has read before and knows that she likes. This is her safe choice. Third is a title she has heard about at school or from a friend. Fourth is her favourite; this one she chooses at random, running her fingers along the spines until she connects with one which just feels right. This is a treasure trove but can be a risk. She encounters William Makepeace Thackeray and Mary Shelley.

She takes home a novel by Aldous Huxley and the librarian asks if her mother enjoyed it. When Claire replies that it was for her, and she wasn't quite sure about its dystopian view of society, Joyce is summoned. She buttons up and heads to the library to be questioned over her daughter's literary preferences. The librarian trembles beneath her withering gaze as Joyce assures her that Claire is old enough to read whatever she chooses, and what exactly do they consider to be 'suitable' reading matter for teenagers anyway? She is secretly proud that her daughter has entered this brave new world.

****

It happens again as Claire stands in assembly. She clenches her thighs tightly together, willing the blood not to come. She feels weak with shame and flushes red then white. She feels a pounding in her temples, a throbbing in her ears, and a flickering in her eyesight. She is going blind as well. There are black spots before her eyes, which when she tries to focus on them, float away to the edge of her vision, waiting to drift back and trip her up.

'There's no discouragement, shall make him once relent
His first, avowed intent…'

She can't concentrate on the words. Elsie looks at her strangely and she topples forward through the throng of navy blue blazers. They part like stormy seas as she pitches headlong to the wooden floor. The sentiments of the hymn mock her as she passes out.

'Who so beset him round with dismal stories
Do but themselves confound; His strength the more is.'

****

She has a bump on her head and has grazed her elbow. Other than that, she feels fine, but rather foolish. She is lying on a hard narrow bed that she thinks is matron's ward. She has never been here before, although she has seen it from the outside. She remembers the blood and hopes that no one has discovered it. She reaches a hand down to touch herself and meets a strange contraption which appears to pass around her waist and between her legs. She gasps involuntarily with fear and surprise.

The curtain is whisked back and there is Miss Partridge. Claire expects her to be cross; she is wasting her time. She struggles to try and get up, but Miss Partridge smiles and lays a hand on her shoulder. She draws up a wooden chair and sits beside the bed.

'Hello Claire, good to have you back with us. You're okay, you just took a bit of a tumble and now you've been having a nice rest. How do you feel?'

Claire smiles wanly and nods. Why is Miss Partridge, her English teacher, here and not Matron? Miss Partridge pours her a beaker of water and hands it to her. Claire sits up to drink it, not realising how thirsty she has become.

'Matron is busy so I said I'd keep an eye on you. We should probably have a little talk. You can stop me and ask questions any time you like.'

Miss Partridge seems to know what she is thinking, and now she is going to tell her about the mystery illness. Her internal organs are falling out, and something has been attached to her to keep them in place.

'Do you know why you are bleeding?'

Claire is scared. She shakes her head and whispers,

'No.' She has tears in her eyes. She doesn't want to hear that she is dying.

But she doesn't. Miss Partridge tells her about menstruation. She talks of blood and migraines, sore breasts and mood swings. She tells her that it happens to all women, even her. Claire blushes at that. She tells her it will happen every month until she gets too old or pregnant. She blushes at that too. Miss Partridge explains about sanitary belts and washable cloth pads. She says they have some at the school. They would like the belt back when Claire has got one of her own, but she can keep the pad. She tells Claire that it comes with the onset of puberty; that her body is ready to have a baby and if one isn't implanted, her body will reject the tissue it has built up, like preparing a spare room for a guest that may one day arrive, and changing the sheets every month until he does.

As Claire listens, she forgets to be scared. She is amazed. She asks how a baby would be implanted. Miss Partridge tells her about sperm and eggs. She tells her about reproduction and making love. She tells her about penises and vaginas. Miss Partridge is gentle and calm. Claire forgets to blush. She thinks her body is wonderful, full of secrets and mysteries.

'And my mother?'

'What about your mother?'

'Does she know all this?'

Miss Partridge laughs, but not unkindly, and she sweeps Claire's hair from her forehead.

'Yes, of course, she does. How do you think you and your sister got here?'

Claire is furious. How could her mother have let her go through this agony; this doubt and fear? Miss Partridge sees her face cloud.

'Don't be too harsh on her. Some people find it difficult to talk about. Some people think it's not an acceptable topic. Maybe, she thought you already knew. You're a very intelligent girl, Claire.'

How could she have known? Miss Partridge is right. People never talk about it. It all makes sense now. She is determined to tell Jean as soon as possible, so that she never thinks she is dying from internal bleeding. She will save her sister that if she can.

Miss Partridge smiles and indicates another chair in the corner of the small room.

'There's a spare skirt for you to put on. Your own is in that bag and needs a wash. Matron says can you bring the other one back when you're ready. It may be a bit big, but it should do for now. 'If you want to know anything, about anything at all, you can always come and ask me.'

Miss Partridge stands to leave.

'Thank you' says Claire, and she means it.

Miss Partridge smiles again.

'You're a woman now, Claire.'

6

Liverpool Street

Zone 1: Central (between Bank and Bethnal Green), Circle and Metropolitan (between Moorgate and Aldgate), Hammersmith & City (between Moorgate and Aldgate East). Connections with National Rail.

Nearby attractions: Lloyd's building; Old Spitalfields market; Petticoat Lane.

Liverpool Street is one of the four railway stations on the London version of the Monopoly board.

It was built on a site which had been occupied by Bethlem Royal Hospital from the 13th to the 17th century and housed the mentally ill.

The station was named after Lord Liverpool, aka Robert Banks Jenkinson, aka Lord Hawkesbury, aka Prime Minister of the United Kingdom from 1812 – 1827 after the assassination of Spencer Perceval.

Situated on the border between the City of London and the East End, Liverpool Street is one of London's busiest commuter stations, in the heart of the city's financial district. Trains from Liverpool Street do not go to Liverpool.

It was the first place in London to be hit by German Gotha bomber aircraft in World War I. One hundred and sixty two people were killed. During World War II a bomb which landed in nearby Bishopsgate completely shattered the glass roofing. In 1993 it was extensively damaged when a Provisional IRA bomb exploded in Bishopsgate. In July 2005, terrorists exploded a bomb on a London Underground train shortly after it left Liverpool Street. Seven people were killed.

Finished in 1986, the Lloyd's building was considered one of the most controversial buildings in London. Like the Pompidou Centre, all the messy but essential services such as lifts, staircases, electricity cables and water pipes were put on the outside to allow for uncluttered spaces on the inside.

****

Claire stands before the headmaster. She has long blonde hair, which she plaits every morning to keep it out of her face. As she sits at her desk, the boys behind pull her plaits and have lately taken to dipping them in their ink wells. Claire whirled round to remonstrate and sprayed a perfect arc of blue/black permanent ink around the classroom. Drops spattered on everything white; notebooks, blouses, and Miss Owens' sallow face. She was marched here, to the headmaster's office, which made a break from the tedium of quadratic equations at least.

Mr Morgan frowns. He removes his glasses and pinches the bridge of his nose. He looks up at Claire and shakes his head. She recognises the clichés of an actor playing the role of a teacher. She wouldn't be surprised if he steepled his fingers. Mr Morgan steeples his fingers.

'Miss Bramblecombe.' He clears his throat as though the effort of remembering her name has quite exhausted him.

'You know why you are here?'

Claire wonders if perhaps he doesn't, but she had to sit outside the door while Miss Owen explained things to him, and she heard voices for long enough so she assumed that he had been primed.

'Not really, sir.'

'Don't be so impertinent, child,' Miss Owens spits. She is Welsh and good at spitting. Mr Morgan waves his hand wearily at her and Claire sees that his exhaustion isn't caused by his pupils at all. He motions for Claire to be seated, which she is, leaving Miss Owens fizzing furiously behind her.

'Thank you, Miss Owens; that will be all.'

'But, I just –'

'Thank you.' He waits until Miss Owens has buzzed from the room, and then, surprisingly, he smiles at Claire. His stern face becomes handsome and kind. Not in the 'poor fatherless child' way that Claire has become accustomed to, but as though he is actually genuine.

'I hear the boys have been teasing you.'

Claire starts. She was expecting a scolding, maybe even the slipper, of which she has heard rumours. Now Mr Morgan looks like he would only use slippers for wearing, perhaps teamed with a smoking jacket and a tot of something expensive.

'Um, yes, sir. They dip my plaits in the inkwells, sir.'

'I heard that. Boys can be horrible little beasts. I remember only too well.' He looks reflective for a second and then shudders out of the memory. He coughs again and leans back.

'Try and understand that boys tend to be childish. They are not as grown-up and sensible as you, and in fact most girls, are. They play games. Especially when they like someone.'

'But, they don't like me, sir. They pull my hair; they push past me in the corridors; they call me 'prickly'; they throw things at me; they hide my gym bag...'

Claire stops and looks down at her hands, clasped in her lap. She has Gone Too Far. She has Told Tales. She glances up to see Mr Morgan nodding and smiling. She wonders fleetingly if he is slightly insane.

'That's how boys show that they like girls, I'm afraid. It's a long way from chocolates and flowers, admittedly, but that's how it all starts.'

Claire stares at him. She is horrified. It can't be true. Those boys who follow her and try to get her attention, and then giggle and run away – is that what this means? They like her? She blushes.

'I told you they were childish. They like you. You are an intelligent and attractive girl and they don't know how to express themselves. You should feel sorry for them, really.'

Mr Morgan is still smiling at her, as though in sympathy. She tries to take it all in.

'But Miss Owens says this is all my fault.'

Mr Morgan laughs a loud, short laugh.

'I'm afraid Miss Owens probably knows as little about male motives as you do, my dear. It's been a long time since anyone dipped her hair in an inkwell.'

He stands and comes around the side of the desk, lifting her out of her chair where she has remained seated and stunned.

'Get matron to find you a clean blouse, and maybe try wearing you hair in a bun for a while?'

Claire stands to leave his office in a daze. He shakes his head again and smiles as she walks down the corridor towards adulthood, and he calls after her,

'Try not to be too hard on them, Miss Bramblecombe.'

****

At the weekends, Claire and Elsie play Monopoly at Elsie's house. They are addicted, but they can't play during the week because Claire has too many chores. Claire has to look after Jean so she comes too. She sits in the corner with Lamby having tea parties and telling her stories. Sometimes she is allowed to be banker and count out the crisp notes, and sometimes Claire lets her roll the dice for her, but Jean is not allowed to play; she doesn't know The Rules.

Claire and Elsie give the streets and stations personalities. Bond Street is a true gentleman in a pin-striped suit and silk handkerchief. Fleet Street is rather vulgar; a scarlet woman with painted lips and nails who pouts and flirts her way to the top. The Angel Islington is a demure nurse of little means and large morals. Mayfair is a cantankerous old goat whom nobody likes, banging his silver topped cane on the floor, coughing up phlegm and shouting at the servants.

Bow Street is a lady of the night; a tart with a heart of gold – the oranges remind Claire of Nell Gwynn. Leicester Square goes to all the right parties in glittering gowns and spends far too much of daddy's money, daahling. Old Kent Road is a barrow boy murdering the cockney vowels with alarming disregard, and Northumberland Avenue is an eccentric lord down on his luck.

Mornington Crescent

There is a strict hierarchy; a Monopoly ladder whose rungs are climbed when the square is landed on. The steps are literally climbed on a bookcase and each time a player lands on the property, the title deed card is raised a shelf. They have to converse with the other personalities on that shelf. Hence Regent Street, the old cad, bribes The Electric Company to turn out the lights so that he can have his wicked way with the innocent factory girl, Pentonville Road. He promises he will put her in the pictures if she shows him more than her petticoats, but her honour is saved by the returning soldier, young Piccadilly, who goes up a level to report the vile deed to her father, the chaplain at Whitechapel Road.

Great sagas are created in the study of Elsie's parents. They don't really care about the game, and often lend each other money when they can't pay their bills – each square keeps its own rent so Park Lane becomes a vicious usurer, while Euston Road is keen to lend £10 to anyone who needs it until the end of the week, no interest me old china, just buy us a pint some day. Claire, who usually ends up owning the dark blues, often turns a blind eye when Elsie lands on Mayfair. She can't concentrate over the sound of his hacking cough and she lets the rent sail by. She declined to buy Coventry Street because she knew that Elsie wanted the set, and now she tiptoes past the hotels in the night, hoping to seek refuge with the kindly Oxford Street who has been known to smuggle her into his club.

The game has gone on for months, and will only end when someone reaches the pinnacle of the bookcase heights. If it is someone they don't like, however, it turns out to be a false summit and more levels are instantly added. They have made their own board and the streets are taken from their local town. Naturally their streets make up the dark blues, and those of the people they don't like occupy the less salubrious districts of the browns and pale blues. This board is too precious to be played with and it sits in its homemade box. When they are famous, they will auction it off at Christies and people will thrill to see their creative innovation. Claire has no idea what she will be famous for. It won't be for her business acumen.

Jean is giggling. They have almost forgotten that she is there and they turn to see what she is doing to amuse herself. She and Lamby are having a tea party but they are not drinking tea. They have been sampling the amber, claret and clear liquids from the crystal decanters, pouring them into the miniature glasses and sipping them like elegant ladies. Lamby has long since keeled over and Jean is waving a minty green glass at her saying,

'Come on, Lamby, it's like mouthwash!'

'Shit!'

Elsie doesn't swear often, but she knows this is serious. If her parents catch them drinking in their study, they'll never be allowed to play again, and they can't leave Northumberland Avenue to rot in debtor's prison.

'Stand up, Jean.'

But Jean just giggles again and then starts to cry.

'I feel sick!'

Taking one arm each, they pull her to her feet, but they can't escape through the front door, because Elsie's parents are in the front room and they can't risk getting caught. There's nothing for it; they'll have to climb out of the window. Claire goes first and Elsie pushes Jean after her.

Jean is howling by now, and hiccoughing at the same time. She sprawls on top of Claire in the rose bushes, tearing her clothes and getting mud all over her. Elsie stays behind to clear up, urging Claire to run and throwing Lamby out behind them. Easier said than done with Jean stumbling and falling beside her. They get away into the bushes where Jean sits sobbing and vomits on the plum tree.

Claire heads home with a dazed Jean under her arm. She has to drag her around the alleys first to try and sober her up. Jean groans and just wants to be left alone to sleep. Claire bullies and cajoles her into walking up and down. It takes hours to cover a few steps, Jean is on her hands and knees, her clothes are a complete mess. Claire finally gets her home and into bed. Joyce, at her keyboard, doesn't seem to have noticed. Claire places a saucepan beside Jean's bed and hopes that she doesn't need to use it.

How can they think they got away with it?

****

Joyce is angry. She hangs up her coat in the hall closet and kicks off her shoes, muttering to herself. Jean looks up at Claire, afraid and relying on protection. Claire waits. Her mother calls her to the kitchen.

'I've just been hauled up in the street by Elsie's mother. Frightful woman.'

Joyce sniffs. This is the ultimate in her expression of disapproval. Being hauled up in the street is common. Claire casts her eyes down, anticipating the lecture about looking after her sister and not letting her get drunk on various spirits in other people's studies.

'She says you had a book.'

'A book?'

Claire is confused. What is this about? What book? Why would she care?

'Yes. An immoral and obscene publication, apparently. Which you gave to her daughter. She says she doesn't want the filth in the house and that you should be punished for trying to corrupt others.'

Claire is still bemused. She has never given a book to Elsie, but if it's as vile as all that, why would Elsie say she has? She looks at Joyce, who is expecting a reply.

'I, um, I suppose I must have lent her something, but I don't remember.'

'Does *The Rainbow* mean anything to you?'

There is a pause while Claire runs through possible answers in her mind. A spectrum of colours? The reflection of the sun in raindrops? The symbol of God's promise to Noah never again to flood the Earth? Somehow, she knows that these aren't the required responses.

'I thought not.' Joyce shakes her head.

'It's a novel by D.H. Lawrence. Not a particularly good one in my opinion, full of tortured prose and unconvincing female characters, but it's got some people very hot under the collar. It's been banned. Elsie clearly has a copy of it, and she thought she'd say you gave it to her. I don't care if you did or not. People who ban books are as bad as those who burn witches. Tell me the truth, Claire. Did you lend it to her?'

'No.'

That seems to be it. No lecture. Nothing. Claire turns to go, but stops and looks back at Joyce.

'If Elsie's going to get into trouble for having a book, can I say it is mine?'

Joyce nods sternly, 'If you want to. But you'll have to read it.'

****

Claire stands before the headmaster, again. He holds a brown paper bag in his right hand. She can see it contains a book, but she's pretty sure it's not *The Bible*. He looks tired for real this time, not like an actor, and he doesn't ask her to sit down. He doesn't ask her if she knows why she's here either.

'There's been a lot of fuss about this book. Miss Wainwright's parents say you gave it to her. Is that true?'

'It's what I said, sir.'

Claire hopes that this doesn't sound flippant. Mr Morgan looks at her over his glasses and nods.

'They say that you are an immoral influence and that you ought to be stopped from influencing impressionable minds. They suggest that I expel you from school.'

'But it's only a book!'

Mr Morgan snaps to attention and flings the book down on his desk. There is no remaining trace of his genial expression. He is shouting.

'No, Miss Bramblecombe, it is not only a book. It is a work of fiction. Someone has bothered to write this and it has received much critical acclaim. Because some people dislike the content, they seek to ban it and stop other people from reading it. They are trying to force their opinion on us. Do you agree with that, Miss Bramblecombe?'

'No, sir.'

'Do you think that people should be able to read what they want to read, without fear of censure and to make up their own minds?'

'Yes, sir.'

'Well, Miss Bramblecombe, it appears that you and I, and, I dare say, your mother, believe in freedom of speech and thought. I will not allow these things to be taken from this school while I am headmaster. Please take your book.'

Claire steps forward to pick up the offending article. Mr Morgan removes it from the clandestine bag and hands it to her. Their eyes meet.

'Am I not expelled then, sir?'

Mr Morgan laughs heartily and leans back in his chair. He waves her out of his office.

'Of course not, Miss Bramblecombe.'

Claire is not allowed to play with Elsie again. Their games of Monopoly come to an abrupt halt. She will never forgive D.H. Lawrence.

7

Mile End

Zone 2: Central (between Bethnal Green and Stratford), District and Hammersmith & City (between Stepney Green and Bow Road).

Nearby attractions: Museum of Childhood; Royal London Hospital; Tower Hamlets.

Mile End takes its name from a milestone signifying the point one mile east from the City of London.

In 1381 the Essex rebels, led by the priest Jack Straw, marched on London to protest against the tax collectors of Brentwood. On 14th June, the young King Richard II met the uprising of 60,000 men at their camp at Mile End and signed their charter.

The Museum of Childhood in Bethnal Green is part of the Victoria and Albert Museum, and contains Britain's largest collection of toys including dolls, dollhouses, trains, cars, rocking horses, puppets, games and costumes. The museum opened in 1872 with vague exhibitions and collections of French art.

When Arthur Sabin became head curator in 1922 he noticed the museum was frequently filled with bored, noisy children, so he decided to make it more child-friendly and began to source child-related objects. He was assisted in his endeavours by Queen Mary (wife of King George V) who donated many of her own toys.

****

Claire squats in the gutter and rolls marbles. She selects each orb from Jean's bag and rotates it slowly through her fingers: tiger eyes; bull's eyes; pop eyes; black eyes; frog eyes; turtle eyes, like dried peas. Spiders; swirls; crystals; pearls; rubies; hotdogs; bird cages; mock melons. Glow worms; corals; hurricanes; panther pits; liberty bells; their combined patriotic tricolour weaving smoky patterns. She admires the colours and the sheen. She loves the sound as they clack together and the smooth spherical shape. Some have little nicks in them as Jean has fired them across rough surfaces to claim her captives.

Jean is a champion marble shooter. Having mastered the art of back-spin, she defeats all challengers, even the boys. Snake eyes are red and black, twisted together like demonic flame. These are the boys' favourites. Cat's eyes are common and dispensable. Claire loves the feline flicker in the centre of the glass. Dead eyes are milky and blind. Shooters are slightly larger and start the game. Jean is unsentimental about individual gems, and she always plays keepsies. Claire spins a shiny globe laced with intricate silver patterns. She would hate to part with this one. It is not her decision. Since being ostracised by Elsie, she no longer plays her own games.

Claire sighs and rakes her fingers through the bag. Jean has given it to her for safe keeping as she skips and sings around the playground, her red curls distinguishing her from the other dervishes.

Mornington Crescent

*'Oranges and lemons
Say the bells of St Clemens.'*

Claire watches them idly as they form a bizarre country-dancing archway to squeeze through. The two girls clasping their hands stand on tip-toe and lean out to give them maximum space. Of course this lowers the bridge and the rest of the girls crouch low, taking their time in the rhyme's early stages, swooping and looping like drunken homing pigeons. The bells of St Martin's, Old Bailey and Stepney whine for their money.

'It's only five farthings, for goodness sake,' Claire thinks as the girls speed up their pattering feet. Shoreditch and the great bell at Bow try to spin out the inevitable, but the money collectors can't be postponed indefinitely.

*'Here comes a candle to light you to bed.
Here comes a chopper to chop off your head.
Chop chop chop chop the last man's head!'*

The girls shriek and wail as they race through the human hatchets, not wanting to be captured. And who would?

****

The air raid siren is a shock, as always. Claire is starting to become blasé, but the first note, as it winds up to a crescendo, makes her stomach somersault.

She grabs Jean's hand and the bag of marbles (wouldn't want to lose those, she thinks wryly) and watches as the girls scatter to their homes and shelters. Calculating quickly, she knows their house is too far away and she tries to think of a communal building where they can take cover. It has been drilled into her to find the nearest shelter, and she is frantically trying to remember where that is. Concentrate. Focus! Everywhere there is wavering and indecision; arguments about which direction is best; what to do; where to run?

She follows a tidal wave of bleak resignation to a makeshift bunker in the church crypt. Down the steps it is dark and smells of earth and sweat. Jean is nervous of the tombs and bodies, and Claire hugs her tightly. She is quiet and still and lets herself be held. A deathly silence settles as no one speaks. Claire can make out a few faces in the glimmering light from the lamp. She sees the fear in the eyes of those who cower with them; shuddering at the rumbles and blasts – a woman seems to be muttering prayers and an old man is rocking back and forth. She thinks, 'We are like animals here, reduced to a dumb herd, waiting for release or execution – a cattle pen; a battery farm'. She hates the people who have done this to them and she absently strokes Jean's hair.

A loud bang rocks them all and is followed by earth raining from above. They hear glass smashing, dogs barking, and bricks tumbling, people screaming – things are falling and breaking apart outside. The praying woman begins wailing and the shelter shudders. Claire is scared. She doesn't want to die here.

****

As the All Clear sounds, the girls race through the streets towards the clouds of smoke, where the loud bangs have come from. People stumble past in the other direction, with crying children and mysterious bundles. The sky is black and there are bodies. Wardens shout and wave but they head blindly towards home.

Claire keeps pulling Jean forwards against the tide like a young King Canute. Sounds muffle and her vision blurs. She sees blood. A woman clutches her head; when she removes her hands they are red and sticky. A man holds his leg, staring at it in wonder.

It becomes eerily quiet as she turns into her street and stops. Jean's howling stops. Everything stops.

'Where's our house?'

It's a fair question. The rest of the street is intact, but the space occupied by their house is smouldering. There is no house, only a devastation of bricks, rubble and destroyed china. The papers will call it a direct hit. Claire feels cold. In this nightmare she walks forward, still holding Jean by the hand, stumbling through rubble. Her mind is screaming in the silence but she refuses to listen to it. A warden stands in front of the spectacle; when he sees them approach, he shoos them away. Claire shakes her head, grimly.

'This is our house.'

'Where?' comes the plaintive cry from Jean. The warden touches his hat in a gesture of respect. Claire has seen it too recently. She clenches her jaw and shakes her head again, more firmly.

'Was there anyone else living here?'

Claire notices the past tense but she won't acknowledge it.

'Yes. Mum.'

It's all she can say, but it is enough. Jean understands and her eyes fill with tears. They look up to Claire and there is the hurt and pain that Claire never wanted to see again. The warden crouches down to Jean and puts his hand on her shoulder.

'What's your name, love?'

As if that matters. Jean doesn't answer him and he looks so uncomfortable that Claire almost feels sorry for him. How often has he done this? How often will he have to? Will it ever get any easier? Will he develop a formula: bad news; crouch; ask name; take to bunker; offer sweet tea; send to orphanage? He looks to Claire, beseechingly.

'This is Jean.

'Okay, Jean. Well, we'll just take you somewhere safe and sort out what happens next.'

'No!' Claire sounds sharper than she meant to. She doesn't even recognise the voice. 'We'll wait here for mum.'

'I'm sorry, love, but if your mum was in there...' He trails off, embarrassed. He can't break this news.

'She wasn't.' Claire wishes she were as sure as she sounds. But this can't be happening. Everything must be okay somehow, it just isn't fair. She is in shock.

She sees someone running towards them and shouting, arms windmilling and mouth open, but she can't hear the words. Jean starts running towards the person, Claire has let go of her hand and she suddenly feels so tired. Not again, she can't have let her sister down again.

But then she sees that the figure has picked Jean up and clasped her in a maternal hug. Claire isn't used to seeing her mother being maternal, but, yes, it's Joyce! Claire walks towards her hesitantly, but Joyce is there and she has gathered her into the embrace and she squeezes them with that fierce mother love that feels like it could break bones.

'Oh, thank God. I was so worried. Thank God you're alive!'

Claire hears these words from a distance and they make their way through to her brain slowly, as though travelling on leaf-strewn tracks. They burst into her consciousness and the sound roars out of the tunnel. The noise is too loud and the colours are too bright and there are tears on her cheeks as she faints.

8

Royal Oak

Zone 2: Hammersmith & City (between Westbourne Park and Paddington).

Nearby attractions: the Idler Academy; the Print Room; the Puppet Theatre Barge.

In 1651, following the Battle of Worcester, King Charles II hid in Boscobel Wood to escape the Roundheads. As he lay concealed in an oak tree, a Parliamentarian soldier passed directly beneath him. The popularity of this story led to Staffordshire potter, Thomas Toft, making large dishes with a design of the 'Royal Oak' supported by the lion and the unicorn and with the king's face peeping from the branches. The tree was destroyed in the 18th century by tourists cutting off branches as souvenirs. The tree now standing on the site is the 'Son of Royal Oak', believed to be a two or three hundred year old descendant of the original. In 2000, Son of Royal Oak was badly injured in a storm and in 2001 an oak sapling grown from one of the son's acorns was planted near the site of the original by Prince Charles.

Opened in 1982, the 55-seat Puppet Theatre Barge presents marionette and rod puppet spectacles based on works from ancient legends, Aesop's fables, and classic fairy tales, to adaptations of Charles Dickens, William

Shakespeare and Frederico Garcia Lorca. Moored at Regent's Canal during the winter, the barge travels up the Thames over the summer months.

As a puppeteer you can perform any role you want and achieve almost invisibility as the audience never look at you directly, but at the character you are manipulating. The magic of the theatre is enhanced by the rocking of the boat as the river slides inexorably past.

HMS Royal Oak was the first battleship to be lost in WWII.

****

Claire is apprehensive as the train pulls in to the station. Joyce has decided that the city is no place for her and her sister, especially as they no longer have a house to live in. Jean's friends with a cottage in the Lake District offer to take Jean with them 'for a while'. Joyce opts to stay near her publishers and has found some distant cousins to look after Claire – she makes it sound as though she has been rummaging down the back of the sofa for them.

The family consists of a girl called Elizabeth, a couple of years older than Claire, and three boys; Edward, William and George. Evidently their mother, Eleanor, is a bit of a monarchist. They own a huge portion of land and a dairy farm by the sea. Their father, Hugh, ran off with the barmaid at the local pub, leaving his wife and children to run the farm on their own.

As she steps on to the platform, she is met by Edward or Eddie as he prefers to be known. He is twenty and taciturn. His dark blond hair is cropped short, although a fringe of curls falls into his bright blue eyes as he slouches against the wall with his hands in the pockets of his overalls. He looks her up and down, his tanned weathered face taking everything in, before he ambles over and takes her suitcase with a curt nod. He introduces himself and turns to leave, expecting her to follow. She has to run to keep pace with his stride.

She stops in disbelief as they turn the corner, but Eddie throws her case nonchalantly into the tractor and then swings into it himself. He looks at her with a hint of amusement as he waits for her to join him. She is wearing a short skirt and curses herself for its inappropriateness. He reaches out a hand which she clasps as he drags her onto the beast. She stumbles and his large hand practically encircles her bare thigh as he steadies her. She gasps and blushes.

There is only one seat and it is clear that she is expected to sit in front of him between his legs. The journey along the bumpy track is excruciating and neither of them speaks. Claire presses her knees together and tries not to be jolted against the rough man behind her. She can feel his body heat and the place on her leg where his hand had been burns as though it was branded.

When they arrive she is awestruck. When Joyce said they lived in a farmhouse, Claire imagined a tumbledown cottage, perhaps with a spray of roses across the front door. This is a huge three-storey building of solid stone set in a small hollow that keeps the sea breezes at bay. Eddie leaves the motor running and stands up. Pushing her forward, he jumps down with her case and holds out his arms to her. She falls down into them and springs away from him. He smells of cows and fresh sweat.

'This is it. Mum's indoors. I've got to get back to work.'

He climbs back into the tractor and rumbles off. Claire takes a deep breath. This isn't what she had been expecting. What had she been expecting? All her second cousins twice removed – or whatever they were – lined up in a neat row, waiting to be presented? She picks up her case and walks to the front door. She pushes it open, feeling foolish.

'Hello?'

'Is that you Claire? Come on in here love; I'm up to my elbows.'

Claire follows the warm and friendly voice along the hallway into a cool kitchen. The description is apt, as there is a woman in there standing over a big bowl of flour, much of which is strewn across the wooden table and on her clothes. She dusts her hands on her apron and holds them out to Claire.

'Well, hello, my lovely. Haven't you grown into a fine looking woman? I'm Eleanor, as you might have guessed. We have met once, but you were a tiny baby at the time so I'll not expect you to remember. I'm sorry my dear, but you've caught me making bread. Where's Eddie gone?'

'Oh, he, um, he left. He had work to do, he said.'

'Great gormless oaf. He's not much good with company. Not that we get a lot of it. At least he met you on time, didn't he?

'Yes, yes he did. Thank you very much.'

Eleanor pushes a wisp of auburn hair back from, her face leaving a floury smudge across her cheek. Claire smiles; she looks so like Jean. And completely unlike Joyce, who Claire can't imagine up to her elbows in anything but paper. Suddenly she feels a long way from home. Eleanor is sympathetic.

'You'll be tired after your journey. I'll get Lizzie to show you your room and you can unpack and have a wash.'

Lizzie appears when called for. She has the same button nose as her mother and a Pre-Raphaelite mane of strawberry blonde hair pulled back into a knot.

'Come on then, you get the attic room. That'll keep you nicely out of the way of us lot!'

Claire follows her up a couple of flights of stairs to a small but neat room on the top floor. The bed is covered with a patchwork quilt and there is a bunch of bright blue cornflowers on the chest of drawers. She looks out of the little window to the sea sparkling below. Lizzie watches her curiously and Claire feels as though she is some bizarre ornament, little knowing that Lizzie has imagined her to be an example of sophisticated city life.

She washes her face and changes into a long skirt and sturdy shoes, mindful of her previous embarrassment. Lizzie takes her for a quick walk around the farm and Claire blushes when she sees the tractor parked in the yard. Awkwardness steals over her as she knows she will have to sit with Eddie at dinner. A boy of about twelve shoots past in a whirring of limbs and a shock of blonde hair.

'That's George. Mad and a farmer; uncanny, don't you think?'

Lizzie laughs to herself as George leaps into the tractor and starts it up. As he reverses, there is an unearthly squeal. George doesn't seem to hear and continues to back up, but Claire rushes to a small heap twitching in the tractor's wake. It is a young tabby cat squirming in the dust.

'Stupid thing,' says Lizzie. 'They like to sit on the wheel arch because it's warm. Looks like it's broken its back.'

Claire crouches beside the panic-stricken cat. She talks to it in a soft, soothing voice, but she knows it can't live. She is still horrified when Lizzie calls to Bill to bring a spade. The young lad arrives with one and motions to Claire to step back. He is roughly the same age as Claire with the same blue eyes as the others, abundant curls of glossy brown hair and a smattering of freckles. Claire averts her eyes as Bill drives the spade cleanly through the little cat and the twitching stops.

Claire is crying as she kneels and cradles its lifeless body.

'What was it called?'

Lizzie shrugs, 'It's just a cat. There are heaps of them about. They catch the mice. We don't name them.'

'Don't you want to bury it?'

'Well, no. They're not really pets or anything.' Lizzie takes the dead cat from Claire's arms and carries it away.

George is not impressed by the touching Pieta scene. 'Oh well, dust to dust.'

'Shut up George!' Lizzie hisses.

It is too much for Claire. She turns to flee inside and runs smack into Eddie. He sees the tears on her face and puts his hand on her shoulder.

'Hey, it's alright. What's the matter?'

Claire can't answer this mildly mocking man and she shakes him off and runs to her room. She wants to stay up there all evening but knows that this would be rude as they are expecting her at dinner. She splashes cold water on her face, brushes her hair and creeps downstairs.

Amid the clamour, Eleanor brings in a huge shepherd's pie full of rich meat and gravy, topped with a crust of golden brown potatoes. Bowls of home-grown carrots and beans sit on the table along with great hunks of fresh bread and pats of butter. Eleanor passes a serving spoon to Claire and indicates she should help herself first as she is the guest.

'Is that all you want?' George asks. 'Are you a sparrow?'

'That's enough, George. She can always have seconds if she wants' Eleanor reprimands.

'Yeah, we're not all greedy pigs like you.' Lizzie smiles at Claire who looks down at her plate. She has no appetite after the incident with the cat but she can't say that; they seem to think she's weird enough already. She picks at her food as the dishes are passed around the table and the room is filled with boisterous talk. She can't even finish her tiny portion, much to George's amusement as he swipes her plate clean with a thick slab of bread.

There is rhubarb crumble and fresh cream for pudding.

'Don't you want that either?' William asks.

'Eddie will be hurt; he whipped that cream with his own fair hands.'

'I'm sorry. I'm just not hungry' Claire stammers. She doesn't want to upset anyone.

'Leave her alone' barks Eddie and he sounds really annoyed. Claire bites her lip to stop herself from crying.

Lizzie senses the tension and begins telling a ghost story about how a friend of hers saw a face at her window at night, even though they were on the second floor.

'Must have been on a ladder' says Bill matter-of-factly.

'Or on stilts' adds George.

'Scoff all you like, it's true. Some departed soul trying to get back in, she reckons' Lizzie insists.

'Like Cathy in Wuthering Heights.' Claire tries to participate but then wishes she hadn't when she sees the blank faces staring back at her. She explains about the Brontës and their passionate novels but she draws no response.

'It's just a book' she finishes lamely.

'We don't get much time to read around here' Eddie says. Claire burns at the put down.

'Yeah well, mine's a true story anyway' says Lizzie.

'Whatever it is, it's your turn to wash up with Billy.'

Claire offers to help, but Eleanor will hear none of it. Not on her first night anyway. There is a roster and Claire will be added to it. There are sounds of crashing pans and laughter from the kitchen. Claire excuses herself early and goes up to bed. Eleanor smiles at her,

'Good night love, sleep well.'

She notices that George ignores her and she barely gets a nod from Eddie.

9

Burnt Oak

Zone 4: Northern (between Edgware and Colindale).

Nearby attractions: Barnet FC Training Ground; Royal Air Force Museum; University of London Observatory.

Burnt Oak tube station is on Watling Avenue, off Edgware Road, originally a roman road known as Watling Street. Once an ancient track between Canterbury and St Albans, used by the Britons, part of it was paved by the Romans, and in the 9th century it was used as the demarcation line between the south-western ruled Anglo-Saxon kingdom, and the Danelaw in the north and east.

Burnt Oak is a vibrant, multi-ethnic suburb in the London Borough of Barnet, south of Edgware. When first used the name referred to an area which was just a field on the eastern side of Edgware Road. There is no evidence that the name means anything other than that there was once a burnt oak tree in the field.

The University of London Observatory is part of the Department of Physics and Astronomy at the University College London. As well as being one of the best-equipped astronomical facilities for student training and research in the UK, it offers public tours of the telescopes and other facilities. However it is only clear enough on one night in three or four to see anything noteworthy.

****

Claire opens her eyes and lies still for a second. She doesn't know where she is and it is an unnerving feeling not to be in her own bed. She remembers and smiles. She is an evacuee. She is somewhere on the South Coast and can hear the pounding of the relentless sea against the cliffs. Yesterday she walked along the narrow paths and day-dreamed of smugglers and secret coves full of bottles of rum and *Jamaica Inn*. She loves the place; it's beautiful in the late afternoon sun as the hills turn all colours and shades from green to purple and she hears the cows lowing above the sound of the waves.

'Don't you just want to stand here and revel in the glory of nature?' she asked Lizzie. Lizzie had looked at her as though she were mad. She is getting used to that look.

She stretches and wriggles her toes under the clean crisp sheets, breathing in the smell of laundry. Then she remembers. She is going home tomorrow. The war is not over, but Hitler has stopped bombing the cities and her mother has sent for her. She has found them a new house to live in and she wants her daughters back. Claire misses Jean and wants to see her again. She feels a twinge of guilt that she doesn't feel the same way about her mother.

She can't lie here and think these thoughts. She pushes back the covers and springs from her bed. As she turns down the corners and absently smoothes out the creases she thinks this is the last time she will do this. Tomorrow morning she will strip the bed as she has been taught. She will not think about lasts.

****

The waves whisper on the shore and the pebbles tumble and clack as they are pummelled and prodded. Claire sits with her arms hugging her knees to her chest, looking out to the sea. It is a mild night and her cardigan is draped over her shoulders. She sees the others further down the beach, laughing and drinking in the moonlight. Billy tells her they usually have a bonfire but this is forbidden now. They would sit around the fire, feeding the flames with driftwood and telling stories, but they don't want to give away their position, so now they just sit around. She still can't get used to the silence – so unlike the city.

It is clear that they are in plain view of any would-be attackers. The Germans could pick them off easily – or capture them and do unspeakable things; Claire has heard stories. She scans the silver sky for rogue planes but sees only wisps of cloud. She hears a crunch before her and is startled to see Eddie. She hopes that it is dark enough to disguise her blushes. He still makes her feel uncomfortable and she doesn't know why. She only really sees him at mealtimes.

'Want a drink?'

He holds out a bottle of cider laced with rum. It makes her throat burn, but she holds out a hand to accept it. He sits down beside her and she hands it back after taking a small swig. He rolls the bottle between his palms and she hears the liquid sloshing against the glass.

'So, you're leaving tomorrow.'

It is a statement, but she nods anyway. Then, in case he can't see her, she says,

'Yes, that's right.'

There is silence as they both stare straight ahead. The bottle passes quietly between them. Claire clears her throat and asks,

'Do you want to go back to the others?'

'No' he says calmly, and there is a touch of laughter in his voice as he asks, 'Do you?'

'No. I mean, yes, in a bit, but I just wanted to be alone for a while.'

'Do you want me to leave?'

She can feel his eyes on her but he makes no move to go.

'No. You can stay if you want.'

She bites her lip at how ungracious this sounds, but he stays, so he must want. He looks back at the sea and he sighs in time with the breaking surf.

'Beautiful, isn't it?'

She is surprised. It is, of course, but she never thought Eddie would be one to notice. He snorts softly as if he has read her mind,

'You think you city folk are the only ones who notice? You think because we live here, we're immune to it?'

'No, I – well, you just always seem so pre-occupied –' Claire trails off.

'I feel the pull of the sea. I want to join the navy. I want to serve my country. I want to protect the island. It feels so vulnerable when you see the shore eroded like this. I feel like such a coward and I can't bear the thought of losing it all.'

He grips the bottle tightly and she feels his frustration. Instinctively, she reaches out to touch his hand. It is warm and clenched and she closes her fingers around it.

'You're protecting it by staying here; looking after the farm and your mother and everyone.'

He nods sharply and turns to look directly into her eyes. 'That's what they tell me. I'm not allowed to enlist. But it doesn't make me want to any less. Dad's gone. Someone has to stay and it has to be me. Billy might take over the farm for a while, but he'll probably get the chance to sign up if this goes on much longer.'

He looks angry and hurt and full of feelings that he can't explain. So much responsibility when all he wants is adventure. He has never said so many words to Claire before, but she knows how he feels. She raises her hand to his cheek and strokes it tenderly.

'I think you're doing a fantastic job' she whispers.

Eddie pushes his face into her caress, like a cat and when he speaks, his breath brushes her fingers.

'Do you really?' He sounds as though her opinion really matters and she says 'of course' as she draws him towards her and rocks him in a gentle embrace.

It is only natural to kiss him and his lips are soft and warm. His large hands slide along the bare flesh of her legs and they burn like they did the first time he touched her. This time it is no accident. His arms are around her and he pushes her back against the beach. Her mouth tears at him, she wants to capture all of this; she may not get another chance. What is she doing? She is leaving tomorrow. She raises her hand to stop him, and he stops but his eyes are locked on hers and the heat of his body weakens her resistance.

'I don't think we should.'

Mornington Crescent

'Should what?' He groans and she knows he wants to do things to her that make her blush, but she wants to do them too and that makes her blush even more.

'We don't really know each other, and we're sort of related.'

'Distant cousins,' he whispers, his lips brushing her ear. She closes her eyes and tries to concentrate.

'You're so beautiful, Claire. I've thought so since I first saw you and all I want is to be with you.'

'But you hardly speak to me!'

'I don't know what to say. I'm afraid that you'll laugh at me; that I won't be good enough for you.'

His tongue slides inside her mouth and protestations melt, ebbing away with the tide.

'I think you're amazing,' she manages to gasp as he runs his hand up her body, cupping her breast. She rises on her elbow and her hair falls into her face. He brushes it back, trailing his fingers through its length.

'Let's take a chance. Why be afraid of it?' He reminds her that there's a war on, time is precious; they need to make this moment count. She mutters about tomorrow. He waves it aside and guides her hand to his groin. She is startled by its insistence.

'We might have been meant for each other. To be or not to be, let our hearts discover.' Her heart is thumping under his fingers which are rubbing her nipples. She arches her back as he presses his knee between her legs.

'Are you sure?' She can hardly breathe. The surf is pounding in her ears and she is racked by waves of passion. He licks the salt spray from her neck and sweeps his fingers lower, over her stomach in ever decreasing circles, homing in on their target.

'Now is the time for it, while we're young. Let's fall in love.'

The breakers crash on the shingle. Claire shudders on the pebbles which the sea will grind down to sand. Lizzie calls;

'We're heading home. Are you coming?'

Eddie laughs. He smiles and kisses Claire. He licks the tip of her nose and pulls her to her feet. He holds her hand and they walk back to the house along the beach, catching up to the others. Eddie drains the remnants of the bottle. He whistles a tune that nags at the edge of Claire's memory. Lizzie gives her a look but says nothing.

Claire leaves the next day. Lizzie and Billy come to the station with Eleanor and they all hug her goodbye. Eddie and George are too busy on the farm. Claire cries all the way home.

10

Angel

Zone 1: Northern (between King's Cross St Pancras and Old Street).

Nearby attractions: Camden Passage Antiques Market; Candid Arts Trust; Sadler's Wells.

The Angel was originally an inn near a toll gate on the Great North Road. The coaching inn was the first staging post outside the City of London and became a local landmark, mentioned by authors from Charles Dickens to Salman Rushdie. It is familiar to many as being the only pub on any version of a Monopoly board – the Angel, Islington.

Traditionally a vibrant centre for liberal journalists, writers and artists, Islington is famous for historical residents including Lenin, Thomas Paine, Joe Orton, the Krays, George Orwell and Walter Sickert, along with other Jack the Ripper suspects.

Because of the distance and depth of the platforms from the entrance, the tube station features the longest escalators in Western Europe.

The Family Records Centre used to provide free access to a wide range of family history material where genealogists and local historians could track down family information. Paper volumes provided anyone interested with the opportunity to look up the Civil Registration of births, marriages and deaths. The centre was closed in 2008 as the work of digitising the records was outsourced to India.

****

Jean opens the door and ushers Matthew inside. It is his first time, so Claire isn't sure about him yet. She is upstairs making herself look gorgeous. She will float down the stairs, pausing in glamorous poses aped from the pictures. Matthew stands nervously with his hands clasped behind his back.

'Can you tell her I'm here?'

Jean shrugs. Claire knows he is here. She has heard him come in. She is already ready, but she wants to make him wait. She likes the power of control. Jean walks to the foot of the stairs and calls up to Claire.

'He's here.'

She returns to the sagging sofa and sits down to continue her survey of Matthew. He hasn't moved, but is looking even more uncomfortable.

'Is your mother in?'

Jean shakes her head. Joyce is rarely in these days. She has meetings to attend with her publishers, and topics to research at the library. The girls catch fleeting glimpses of her looking fraught and weary. Claire makes her dinner but other than that they have little contact. There is no need for Matthew to know any of this. He begins to fidget.

Claire appears looking stunning.

'Sorry to keep you waiting.'

She isn't. Matthew's eyes light up and he has to stop himself from licking his lips. He has heard things about her from the other lads and thinks his luck might be in tonight. He picks up her coat from the arm of the sofa and helps her into it. He places a hand in the small of her back and steers her to the door. He is alarmed to see that Jean is buttoning up her own coat.

'Hang on a minute. Where's she going?'

'She's coming with us of course.' Claire's voice is all tender concern. 'Our mother's out and I can hardly leave her in on her own, can I?'

Matthew sighs heavily. He wasn't prepared for little sisters. He tries to put his arm around Claire as they walk to the cinema, but she moves away and holds on to Jean's hand, chattering away to her and ignoring him. It is no better when they get to the pictures. Matthew doesn't mind paying for Claire, especially when he might get something out of it, as he has been led to believe, but he draws the line at paying for her sister. Neither of them produce any money, however, so he buys all three tickets and hopes it is worth it.

They are late and have missed the dark privilege of the back row seats.

'Have you got any cigarettes?'

Matthew hasn't. He doesn't smoke, and his parents would kill him if they thought he did. He doesn't want to look gauche though, so he sneaks back out to the foyer and buys a packet. He slides his arm along the back of Claire's seat, trying to look nonchalant. She takes a cigarette and offers him one, which he takes as casually as possible, although this means removing his arm. He is disconcerted as she continues to look at him with raised eyebrows, waving her unlit cigarette. He realises he has forgotten to buy matches and silently curses his stupidity.

Claire turns round to a good-looking man behind them, who seems only too keen to cup his hand around a tiny flame as she leans in and closes her eyes to inhale. Matthew tries to light his cigarette from hers, but he doesn't know what he's doing and ends up choking, feeling foolish. Within seconds it goes out and he drops it on the floor and hopes she won't notice. He returns his concentration to the matter in hand. Claire leans back and he repositions his arm. She doesn't seem to mind so, after sitting rigidly for ten minutes, he drops his hand onto her shoulder.

Jean shrieks with laughter and he leaps into the air and jerks his arm back. He tries to cover the gesture by scratching his ear. Although the film is a comedy, he is sure Jean only laughs at inappropriate moments when he has worked up his courage to execute a manoeuvre. Matthew tries to ignore her, and he places his hand on Claire's knee. She lets it sit there, motionless for a while as he contemplates his next move. When he inches his fingers up her thigh, she swats him away like an inconsequential insect. When he tries to whisper in her ear, she turns to explain a plot development to Jean, leaving him wreathed in smoke.

At the intermission Claire takes Jean to the toilets and perches on the edge of the hand basin.

'I don't know whether to feel sorry for him or to slap his face! He tried to kiss me before. Just because they pay for you to go to the pictures, they think you owe them something. Well, I don't. The pleasure of my company should be enough reward.'

Jean sighs. Although Claire is laughing, Jean knows she is serious, she has heard this particular lecture many a time.

'So, am I staying?'

Claire nods and blows smoke up to the ceiling. Sometimes she would send Jean home at this point if

Mornington Crescent

she wanted to be alone with her date, but she is a bit concerned about Matthew's groping hands and she would like her miniature chaperone.

'Yes, let's change.'

Claire stubs out the cigarette and springs from the basin, straightening her skirt, which has ridden up her thighs. They return to Matthew as the film begins again and swap seats. He is horrified to find himself seated next to Jean. As he tries to lean over her to ask what is going on, Claire is engrossed in the film. He repeats himself more loudly and earns shushes from Jean and the good-looking chap in the row behind. He gives up and sits fuming with arms folded.

He doesn't even get Claire to himself afterwards. Jean prattles about the film and Matthew scuffs and scowls as he walks them home. At the door, Claire undoes the top two buttons of her blouse and reaches inside for the key that she keeps on a chain around her neck. Matthew is mesmerised by her cleavage – she has got magnificent breasts and he longs to nestle between them, envious of the key which she slides into the lock. Jean pushes inside and Claire turns to look at Matthew through lowered lashes.

'Thank you so much for taking us out tonight, Matthew. We had a lovely time.'

She raises her eyes to his face and he flushes a deep scarlet. He takes a step towards her and when she doesn't back away, he is emboldened to try and kiss her. He is clumsy, but she puts her hand on the nape of his neck and draws him close. She kisses him passionately and he feels her tongue flicker over his lips. He opens his mouth and pushes his tongue into her warm, smoky mouth. He can feel her breasts against his chest through the thin cotton and he presses close to her body. She senses his eager erection and his hands start to roam over her body. She pushes him away and bites her lip seductively.

'Thanks again, Matthew. I'd better get going.' and she is gone.

Claire goes upstairs to their bedroom, sits on the edge of her bed and brushes out her long hair. Joyce still isn't home and Jean is already in bed, the sheets pulled up to her chin. Claire sighs and turns out the light before slipping between the covers.

'Will you be seeing him again?'

'Probably not. He's a terrible kisser and his hands are sweaty. Besides, I quite like that Barry at Woolworths and he's asked me out a couple of times.'

Jean nods in the dark. She is used to Claire's dismissive ways. She never seems to care about the boys who take her out and she laughs at their romantic gestures and intense poetry. It is just a game to her, but Jean isn't even sure if she likes playing. She lies awake for longer than Claire, thinking about the film. She knows that Claire is fast asleep without a thought of Matthew in her dreams.

****

Matthew walks home with his hands rammed firmly into his pockets. His mind is full of thoughts of Claire and he can barely walk straight. There is an ache in his groin that he can't wait to do something about in the privacy of his own bedroom. He thinks of her lips and her tongue and her breasts and her thighs. He is sweating. Just wait until he tells the lads about this. He wonders how far he can say they went. It's not as if she hasn't already got a reputation.

11

London Bridge

Zone 1: Northern (between Bank and Borough) Jubilee (between Southwark and Bermondsey).

Connections with National Rail and riverboat services.

Nearby attractions: The Golden Hinde; London Bridge; The London Dungeon.

A bridge has existed on this site over the River Thames for over 2000 years. The first one was built by the Romans out of wood in 46 AD. It has been burned and destroyed by storms and bombs and reappeared in many incarnations. London Bridge was the only bridge in London until Westminster Bridge was opened in 1750.

It has been the site of houses, chapels, shops and water wheels. It has displayed the severed heads of traitors and inspired the words of a nursery rhyme. In 1722, to ease congestion, the Lord Mayor decreed that "All carts, coaches and other carriages coming out of Southwark into this City do keep all along the west side of the said bridge: and all carts and coaches going out of the City do keep along the east side of the said bridge", originating the tradition of driving on the left.

One embodiment of the bridge was made of Dartmoor granite and opened in 1831. It was widened in 1904 to *allow for more traffic, but the weight made the bridge sink. By 1924 the east side of the bridge was four inches lower than the west side and it was sold to the American entrepreneur, Robert P. McCulloch for US$2.5 million. He vehemently denied that he thought he was buying the much more impressive Tower Bridge, which is often incorrectly thought of as 'London Bridge' by tourists.*

****

Claire drums her fingers on the table. The movement rattles the teacups in their saucers. She has set everything out and she waits for her mother to come home. Jean is outside with a friend. The clock ticks on the mantelpiece. The teapot squats in the middle of the table brooding beneath its cosy.

Miss Partridge offered to come and talk to her mother if that would make things easier, but Claire doesn't think that it will. She hears the front door open and she takes a deep breath.

Joyce slips out of her coat and hangs it on the wooden hook in the closet. She puts her shoes neatly in the rack and steps into her slippers. She has been at a meeting with the publishers. It went well and she hums to herself as she comes through to the kitchen. She senses something is wrong and sits down at the table, drawing her gloves off slowly and waiting for Claire to speak.

'Would you like some tea?'

'Yes, please.'

The formal air is belied by Claire's shaking hand as she picks up the teapot and pours a stream of liquid into the cups. The two of them sit opposite each other like strangers. Joyce lays her gloves on the table where they curl like shed skin.

'Mum, I need to tell you something.'

Joyce nods and pours milk from the jug into her cup. She spoons in two sugars and stirs. She places the spoon on the saucer and sips. Her mind flickers over engagement and rejects it – the boy would be here. She imagines pregnancy and shudders slightly. She says nothing; she doesn't help.

'As you know, I've done really well at school this last year, and I've got good marks in my exams.'

Claire wills her mother to look at her, wanting praise or at least acknowledgement, but nothing comes. She ploughs on.

'I've applied to teaching college and I've been accepted. The course starts next week.'

She begins to wish Miss Partridge had come after all. There is a silence that she isn't sure how to fill. Joyce takes another sip of tea but she doesn't look up.

'Where?'

This is the bit that Claire has been dreading and it has come so suddenly. There have been no congratulations and there won't be now.

'London.'

The capital sticks in her throat and she has said the word so softly that she isn't sure that Joyce has heard. The clock ticks and Joyce looks at her.

'No.'

'No?'

'No.'

It is not what Claire has expected. She doesn't understand.

'What do you mean?'

'I mean 'no'. You're not going to London.'

Joyce stands and walks calmly to the sink where she rinses the teacup and turns it upside down to drain. She begins to leave the room as though the conversation is over. Claire is suddenly angry. She will not have her dreams dismissed so easily.

'I am, mum. I've won a scholarship, so we won't have to pay. I'll find some nice girls to live with and I'm going to become a teacher.'

The words tumble out. Joyce folds her arms and looks coldly at her.

'You are going to stay here and run the house, and look after your sister. I'm busy and I can't do it myself. I need you to help out. You can study here or do correspondence or something until your sister's old enough to take care of herself.'

Claire stands abruptly and the chair clatters over. Joyce doesn't flinch.

'What about what I need?'

'What do you need? I feed you, I clothe you, I've brought you up alone, and this is how you repay me? I've worked hard and it hasn't been easy. You expect to just leave and abandon all your duties? I don't think so, Claire. We all have to make sacrifices.'

It is Claire's turn to refuse.

'No. I won't do it. I love Jean. And I love you. But I won't stay here and rot. I've got a chance to make something of myself. You have to understand, mum.'

'I understand.'

Joyce looks sad and old and tired. She steps towards Claire and takes her face in her hand. She is going to tilt her chin up to examine her closely, but the two women are the same height now. She looks into Claire's eyes and says almost gently,

'If you leave, don't ever come back.'

****

Claire carries a small suitcase to the bus station. She has left without saying goodbye to Jean. Jean has cried so much and begged her not to go that she doesn't think she can bear the final parting. She has promised to write and told her she can come and visit any time. Joyce hasn't spoken to her. She meant what she said and Claire flees the house without looking back. She won't go back.

She boards the bus and shuffles to the rear. Miss Partridge has recommended a boarding house and made the arrangements. The address is in her bag although she knows it by heart. It is her future on paper. She sits and hopes the bus is empty; she doesn't want to talk to anyone. She turns her face away from the aisle so that she doesn't have to make eye contact.

She sees a small white face with tear tracks staring at her. Jean has come to the station to see her off. Claire hadn't told her which bus she was on, but she must have found out. She is pleased despite herself. She didn't want to leave like this. Alone. And then she sees Joyce standing there too, nodding with a brief smile and a mountain of determination. Claire reaches out her hand to wave goodbye, but only touches her own reflection. She gasps in shock. She looks so young. And so forlorn. The bus shudders into life and the image breaks up.

12

Piccadilly Circus

Zone 1: Bakerloo (between Oxford Circus and Charring Cross), Piccadilly (between Green Park and Leicester Square).

Nearby attractions: London Trocadero; Soho; Criterion Theatre; St James's Church.

A local dressmaker grew rich in the 17th century creating frilly collars called piccadills or piccadillies, an item which gave its name to the famous central London landmark. At the junction of five busy streets, ablaze with electric and neon displays, and situated at the heart of London's entertainment and shopping areas, it is a popular meeting place and tourist attraction.

The Shaftesbury memorial fountain and statue was erected in 1892 to commemorate the philanthropic works of the Earl of Shaftesbury. The winged archer is the first statue to be made of aluminium, which was a rare and precious metal at the time. Often called Eros, after the Greek god of love, it was designed by Alfred Gilbert as Eros' twin, Anteros, the god of selfless love as opposed to his brother, 'a frivolous tyrant'.

When the monument was unveiled, there were numerous complaints, as the use of a nude figure on a public monument was considered controversial. Despite attempts to name the statue The Angel of Christian Charity, it has remained widely known as Eros, which seems appropriate considering its proximity to Soho, and has become a London icon and the symbol of the 'Evening Standard' newspaper.

****

James Burns is like no one Claire has ever met before. She has had a lot of boyfriends and they have all been the same. Tight black polo-necked jumpers; often wearing glasses; smoking cigarettes; drinking cheap wine and talking about politics and literature, waving their arms heatedly and raising their voices to argue about existentialism.

James is different. She met him on a bus and he asked her if she wanted a drink. She surprised them both by saying 'yes'. He makes her laugh, sometimes even with him. He rides a motorbike and goes rock-climbing. He wears scruffy jumpers with holes in them and his battered trousers are often held up with string. He has wild hair which stands on end when he rakes his hand through it. He has a beard which he never trims. He doesn't care what it looks like, he has more important things on his mind.

He 'does' physics. His eyes gleam as he sits at the rickety kitchen table and draws diagrams in the sugar bowl to explain. Claire's friends find him exasperating and they roll their eyes when he comes to visit. He turns down offers of cigarettes and wine but he looks longingly at any leftover food or baking. Claire feels a strange impulse to look after him. She watches him play football, shivering on the muddy sidelines as grown men who should know better run around a claggy pitch after a sodden ball.

When they walk down the street together, he skips ahead, walking backwards so he can watch her while he talks. She doesn't understand half of what he says, but she loves the passion in his eyes. He has no time for the world-weary cynics who file down the hallway in the flat, filled with ennui at eighteen. He takes her to pubs with bands in the corner. He drinks pints of bitter and smacks his lips in appreciation of its simplicity. He will hold it up to the light and look at her through the glass. If she asks about the bubbles in the glass or the brewing process, he will tell her. In detail. When he gets excited, he spills as much as he drinks. She yearns for him to feel that passion for her.

He takes her to dinner at grimy little cafes with sauce bottles on wipe-clean tables that haven't always been wiped clean. He considers this a date. If she asks him to pass an apple, he asks if she wants a googly, a leg-break or a Chinaman. These, she has learned, are cricketing terms and involve an elaborate display of finger and forearm manipulation. The result is always the same, and she usually drops the delivery, at which he smacks his forehead and yells something about a wicket keeper.

She takes him to nightclubs and parties, where he shrinks and looks awkward. Most of her friends aren't interested in the off-side rule or calculating the speed of light, and he's no good at telling jokes. His thoughts spill out of him before he has time to consider their audience. He sits on the stairs nursing a glass of some revolting homebrew and talking to the house dog, or it could possibly be a stray. The dog sits and listens in exchange for a scratch behind the ears, and Claire thinks that is not such a bad deal.

Sometimes they go to the theatre. They queue up on the night of the performance and get tickets if there are any cancellations. They can't afford to book in advance, so they take their chances. If they don't get in, they walk around London, crossing and re-crossing the river, listening to the sounds of laughter and music, smelling the wafts of food and watching twinkling reflections in the sluggish water. She rides on the back of his motorbike as he weaves through the back-streets and she shivers with history. She loves the big city, and he has grown up here and enjoys showing it off, even though her eyes are shut tight. He is careful with his postillion passenger. He is proud to know the word postillion.

They see some stunning plays and revues and experimental theatre. They roar with laughter at Gilbert and Sullivan, and Claire cries at George Bernard Shaw and Henrik Ibsen. They admire Wilde, Rattigan and Barrie, but neither can see the point of Eugene O'Neill. They see some absolute stinkers. James sleeps through students in tights strangling Shakespeare and Claire nudges him awake for the bows. They sit upstairs in the Gods. They may be able to look down on the action, but the seats are uncomfortable.

****

Claire is good at studying. She discovers a talent for explaining. She is calm and patient and the tutors praise her. She does well at exams, in fact she enjoys them. She hates the bit beforehand with everyone pretending they haven't done enough work and building themselves up into a state of tension. She knows it will be okay. She has attended every lecture, read every book and completed every exercise. She is methodical in her approach; she knows what it is she wants to do.

She pictures herself teaching infants. She wants to make a difference. She knows that there are teachers who do. In her vision she wears a cape and sweeps down hallways, holding timid children by the hand and introducing them to the delights of learning. Her door will always be open and she will read stories and write simple equations on blackboards. 'My name is Miss Bramblecombe' she will say and she will underline it in chalk as the high-pitched response rolls back, 'Good morning Miss Bramblecombe'. She will set homework that is fun and she will help anyone who needs it. Parents will come and see her on parent teacher evenings, grateful for her input, and the walls will be hung with bright coloured pictures and messes of papier mâché.

PART TWO

1

Now that she has started crying, Jean is unable to stop. Why the hell did she come to this awful country in the first place? Of course, she knows the answer to that really, but she enjoys indulging in melancholy and rhetoric.

It was horrid when Claire went to London and sent glowing reports of all the fun she was having; the friends she had made; the galleries she was visiting; the plays she was seeing; the nightlife; the culture; the sophistication. Jean was stuck at home being buried alive. She appreciated all that Claire had done, because now she had to do it herself, but she is no saint like Claire and certainly no martyr. It isn't fair! She is the youngest born to a life of adventure, not this endless drudge.

So she placed an advert in one of the higher class of periodicals, promoting herself as 'fit, healthy, adaptable, neat and presentable, of modest habits, and with a great fondness for children'. A family living in New York City answered and Jean packed her bags immediately, telling her mother that she had always wanted to travel and that nothing was going to stop her, although actually, no one had tried.

Now she wishes they had, as she heaves great dramatic sobs onto the counterpane and wishes herself thousands of miles away. Her darling little charges are, quite simply, brats. She has no experience with children and they know it. She has no control over them and they know that too. Perhaps they can smell her fear, like dogs. Even if she admitted she had made a terrible mistake, there is no one she can ask for advice. It's awful all the time, but today has been the worst and she has had enough.

Jean got up as usual at some ridiculously early hour, a problem in itself as she was never what you might call a morning person. She had the familiar struggle of getting Jack and Beth dressed and force-feeding them breakfast as they screamed, bit and kicked. She stuffed them into their coats, cramming mittens onto fists and hats onto heads; then fetched the dog which was cowering by a suspicious puddle in the corner.

The stupid thing looks more like a nailbrush than a dog. It is meant to belong to the children, but they hate it and refuse to take it for walks, so Jean has to drag it around with her when she takes the children to and from school, posts the letters or gets the shopping. She might be more sympathetic towards it if it didn't demonstrate its lack of housetraining at every available opportunity.

Jack raced ahead, keen to get to school and play with his friends, although Jean wonders how the selfish little brat manages to keep any. She shudders at the thought of all the other eight-year-old monsters in his class. Beth dragged her feet, scuffing her new shoes, wailing that she didn't want to go and sitting down on the pavement as she did every morning until Jean wanted to shake her. The dog hid behind every blade of grass.

'I'm just as embarrassed to be seen with you,' Jean thought as she looked at it imitating a wet sponge at the end of a lead, not that she had ever seen one of these, but she felt sure this is what it would look like.

She delivered Jack to his school and frog-marched Beth to hers. She had tried asking about her friends, what she liked doing, what games they would play, but all she ever received in return were sullen glances, so she gave up on the social niceties. When she deposited Beth at the playcentre, however, she began a formidable wailing which terrified the dog, and drew icy glares from the other mums.

Returning to the apartment she heard low voices from the living room. This means that Jules is entertaining. Jules doesn't work, but she has no time for domestics as she is busy doing lunch and chairing committees. This morning she appeared to be practicing her strokes with the young tennis instructor. Jean began to wash the breakfast things when Jules sashayed into the kitchen.

'Oh, you're back. I'm busy right now and we don't really want to be disturbed, so leave that for now. Perhaps you could run along to the shops and get whatever we need?'

They both know that Jean did the shopping yesterday and the scepticism must have been plain. Jules took a couple of notes from her purse and thrust them at Jean.

'Why not get yourself a little treat?'

Jules' voice was brittle with a slightly desperate edge. Jean said nothing but took a long time before she accepted the money, allowing Jules to feel awkward as she proffered it. As Jean left the house she heard the tinkle of laughter and Jules called,

'Take your time, no rush.'

Jean wandered in and out of shops for a few hours. She examined shelves of hair care products, wanting to exchange the sweaty money in her palm for long glossy locks. From the arched eyebrows and pursed mouths of the sales assistants she soon realised the futility of this plan. She saw her frizzy reflection in the polished windows and sighed. She sat on a park bench reading a book until her fingers went numb and her nose dripped onto the pages.

There was silence back at the apartment and a scrawled note asking Jean to change the sheets. She also removed the empty wineglasses from the bedside table. She washed and dried and hung out and put away and swept and polished. She prepared dinner for the children, which she knew they wouldn't eat. Their mother would assuage her guilt by distributing chocolate biscuits. She collected Jack and Beth from school. Beth howled when she saw her and clung to the teacher's leg. She saw the other mums mutter through the horizontal slits in their faces as she prised Beth's fingers away. Jack ran home without stopping at the road crossings and the dog peed in the hallway.

After the battle of the dinner table and supervising the toy fights, Jean made the children get changed and ready for bed. They were in their pyjamas and presented to John when he got home. He tucked them in and read them a story. Jules went to bed early with a headache. John gave Jean an armful of his shirts. She had ironed them incorrectly and he wanted them 'done over'. Thinking whom she'd like to do over, she threw them at her bed, where they lie crumpled now underneath her.

She pauses for breath. She is miserable; this is not what she came here for. So what did she come here for? To have a good time and enjoy new experiences. To have something exiting to put in her letters home. This is New York for heaven's sake; one of the most exciting cities in the world! She sees the money that Jules gave her lying on the bed. She stuffs it into her purse with a lipstick and the front door key. Okay, she'll go and treat herself.

2

Jean hates jazz. She just doesn't see the point. Sure, it's probably all very clever and everything, but she sees it as the devil's music. A perfectly good tune is ruined by people fiddling about and blowing their own trumpet and banging their own drum, as it were. Satan is up there on the saxophone now, squeezing all the recognisable melody out of the piece. It squeals and torments as random sounds spill out of the singer.

Still, this seems an inviting place, and she likes the thumping rhythm of the double bass. She sits in a corner squinting against the smoke, which stings her eyes. She drinks a tall glass of champagne; the bubbles delight her. The combination of music, loud voices, warmth and genuine laughter drew her inside, and now she surrenders to them. As the band finish their set, she leans back into the leather embrace of the armchair and closes her eyes. Smoke swirls around her as her mind empties of all the slights of the day.

'Excuse me, ma'am, can I get you another drink?'

Jean opens an eye and sees the waiter standing over her. She calculates that she has enough for one more glass if she walks home instead of getting the bus. It's a long way, but she's in no hurry and she likes it here, so she nods.

'Yes, please; more champagne.'

How thrilling. Through the haze, she watches the waiter walk to the bar and lean casually against it, smiling at people rushing to talk to him. He orders the drinks and pays for them. Jean sits up straight. He isn't the waiter. But why is he familiar then, she doesn't know anyone here, and why would he offer to get her another drink? And how could she have accepted? And how rude must she have seemed? She begins to panic as he walks back with her champagne and bourbon in a short chunky glass. A quick wave of nausea threatens as she is transported to Elsie's house and the plum tree, but she fights it back.

He slides along the sofa next to her and places the drinks on the table.

'Thanks. I, um, didn't know…, I mean, I thought you were…, um, thank you. Do you want…'

He reaches over and touches her hand to stop her rummaging in her purse. He shakes his head, but he is smiling and she feels he is strong and gentle.

'No, that's fine. I just thought I'd like to come and get to know you a little, if that's okay?'

'Yeah, um, there's not much to know, though. Sorry.'

He laughs and she blushes. She is making such a mess of this. Claire would know what to do. But he looks so kind. He has wide cheekbones, which make his face look open and honest. He looks different, strong, exotic, ethnic. His black hair falls into his eyes and he brushes it back. She feels a strange desire to reach out to that glossy raven's wing and she shudders to shake the thought from her head. His eyes are almost black too, but then it is dark in here.

'Why don't we start with your name?'

'Okay.'

'Well, what is it?'

'Oh right, yes, it's, um Jean.'

The corners of his eyes crinkle and he holds out his hand.

'It's very nice to meet you, um Jean. I'm Henry. My friends call me Hal.'

She takes his hand, which is large and warm and slightly rough. Touch seems so much easier than words. She knows she should have asked him his name before he told her, but she doesn't know whether she should call him Henry or Hal. She wants to appear sophisticated, but not presumptuous.

'Hi' she whispers.

He is looking at her with a smile in his eyes and she tries not to bite her lip. He gestures to a packet of cigarettes he has placed beside his drink.

'Do you mind?'

'Sure, be my guest.'

Jean has picked up this idiom recently, as she desperately wants to fit in, but as she says it here in this club she has never been to before, to someone who seems to know everyone but she can't place, she thinks how incongruous it sounds. He gives a small laugh and looks down. She follows his eyes to see that she is still grasping his hand. She lets go abruptly and sends his glass flying in her haste. He must think she is so stupid. She fumbles and fusses, trying to wipe up the spill.

'It doesn't matter. Do you smoke?'

He holds out the cigarette packet and she takes one. Of course she doesn't smoke, but how can she admit that? She wants to prolong contact with this man, but he's not going to stay for her witty repartee or elegant moves. He strikes a match and she watches his long fingers cup the flame. When he holds it out, she remembers what to do and she leans in to draw the light up and into her. Determined not to cough, she holds the smoke in her mouth for what she deems a suitable length of time, before exhaling discreetly. Should she hold it between thumb and forefinger or middle and index? If only she had practiced. She glances around to see what other people are doing, and settles on placing it in the ashtray. The smoke spirals directly into her eyes and she wants to wave it away but that would look gauche.

Henry/Hal takes a long drag on his cigarette and blows the smoke up past his exquisite lashes. He sighs and licks his lips. Jean is thinking she would like to do that. He startles her by talking.

'So, I don't think I've seen you in here before. Are you having a good night?'

'No. I mean, yes. I um haven't been here before. But it's nice.'

Nice? For heaven's sake! He looks around as though seeing the place for the first time.

'Yeah, not a bad joint.' His eyes return to her and he smiles. His teeth are so white and clean in the gloom.

'I'm English.' He nods. Perhaps he's thinking that this explains everything so she hurries on.

'I'm working as a nanny. It's horrible. I wanted to get away. I thought this might help.'

'Does it?'

'Yes. I'm not sure about the music, but the people seem nice.'

He throws his head back and laughs. Jean doesn't know what she has said that's so funny, but she likes to think that she has engaged him. She picks up the cigarette and knocks the ash from its tip, quite expertly she thinks. He swallows what's left of his drink in a single gulp and stands up. She has frightened him off.

'I've got to get going. Will you still be here in an hour or so?'

She shrugs.

'Maybe.'

He stands and goes to the bar. She has blown it. He is asking the barman for something. The barman looks over and she feels foolish and self-conscious. They will laugh at her later. She stubs the cigarette out, grinding it until there is no more smoke, and drains her glass. Then he is there at her side again with another glass of champagne and a pen and paper.

'Please stay. And if you can't, please give me your number.'

She laughs. She can't believe it. She prints her name and number and hands it back to him. He looks at it closely before folding it and slipping it into his back pocket. The band is back and she watches in horror as Henry/Hal slides his long legs and deliciously tall body behind the drum kit. He picks up a drumstick and waves it at her, his eyebrows raised and a mocking smile on his lips. So that's why he seemed familiar. But he was hiding behind the drums so how could she be expected to recognise him? He says something to the singer who looks at her and laughs.

She is embarrassed and angry. Her eyes are smarting and her throat is burning; she is not sure whether from tears, humiliation, or simply the unaccustomed smoke. She knows she is not going to sit around and wait for more. She leaves her drink untouched and runs out onto the street. The mocking strains of the jazz standard float in her wake.

'I get no kick from champagne.'

3

He calls.

He takes Jean out, away from the apartment. She leaves the affairs and the ironing and the sullen silences behind. The bickering children and the tantrums and the incontinent dog are forgotten as she visits new worlds.

He takes her to the park. He spreads a rug on the grass and produces a hamper. He tries to make cucumber sandwiches but he doesn't remove the crusts or cut them into triangles. He pours champagne and asks her about herself as she lies back under the trees and looks up at the tight buds unfurling at the tips of the branches. He pinches the bread in his paws and she thinks of teddy bears.

He rows her to the middle of the lake and she trails her fingers in the water. Droplets of laughter scatter brilliance through the air. He is strong and competent with the oars. She stands at the stern like Captain Ahab and points. It is a game and she is no longer afraid to rock the boat.

She confesses that she doesn't smoke. He had guessed. He tells her that he prefers a pipe and she leans against him, breathing in the smell of soap and tobacco.

When it rains they run to shelter and he teaches her to play chess. She likes the horses. She likes the way they can charge through the field to the rescue, jumping over obstacles. He tells her that she must protect the King and not worry so much about the knight. The poor Queen has to dash all over the board in all directions while the King can only take one faltering step. She hates sacrificing the pawns. She learns to castle and she does it whenever she can. He tells her these pieces are called rooks in America. She imagines them as birds swooping across the black and white squares of the kingdom. He always wins, but she is happy if she keeps her horses.

He takes her to a Chinese restaurant. There are streets of them with garish signs and indecipherable characters. Their names conjure mythical dragons, exotic blooms and magnificent palaces. She doesn't recognise the food so he makes suggestions: dim sim; wontons; chow mein; Peking duck. The dishes are arranged in the middle of the table and she breathes in the tantalising steam. They eat with chopsticks, which he handles deftly, although they look like tiny toothpicks in his giant hands, spearing the choicest slivers of meat and translucent slices of ginger. They are far less pliant with her and the tablecloth is soon splattered with edible debris. He feeds her from his chopsticks, dangling the morsels into her mouth. She cups the bowl of water with slice of floating lemon and drinks it. He watches her and does the same, so as not to embarrass her.

She calls him Henry. He likes the sonorous tone of her accent. She goes to the clubs where he plays. She still doesn't like the music, but she is right; the people are nice. She likes them all, even Freddie, the tempestuous trumpeter who thinks he is in charge. The band throws in a song every set for her. 'Can't Take That Away From

Me'; 'The Very Thought of You'; 'I Only Have Eyes for You'; 'Yes, Sir, That's My Baby'; 'The Most Beautiful Girl in the World'. She blushes and laughs. It is ridiculous. The band has a following of glamorous girls with long legs, silken hair and perfect teeth, who glare at her unruly auburn curls and too many freckles.

Sometimes she drinks champagne, but mostly not. They can't afford it. Henry doesn't get paid much as a musician. By day, he is an apprentice builder. He promises one day he will build her a dream home. She does not want to be put in an ivory tower. She pictures a rambling villa by the sea with horses and more children than she can count.

They play tennis, wearing crisp whites and vaulting the net. Mixed doubles with Freddie and his girl; there are many. They swig beer from long necked bottles at the drinks' break. Henry gets cross when Jean stands staring at wisps of white in the sky instead of receiving serve. Once when they are losing, she puts Freddie off his serve by flashing her breasts at him. It is out of character but it works. He double-faults for the rest of the game.

Henry takes her to barbecues where the meat is overcooked and the mayonnaise is really salad cream. He introduces her to his friends who all adore her and tell him that she is charming. They celebrate Fourth of July but not May Day; Thanksgiving but not Guy Fawkes. Remember, remember.

She mentally composes letters home to Claire telling her all the wonderful aspects about her man. Sometimes she even sends them. She tells Jules she is leaving. John threatens to hide her passport so that she can't escape. Henry comes round and has words. Jean doesn't know which ones, but her things are thrown out onto the doorstep.

They move in together. She finds work as a secretary. Her typing is slow but she makes a good cup of coffee. He gives up the band. Too many late nights stop him concentrating at work. He says he wants to climb the ladder of construction and frowns when she laughs.

They make love with enthusiastic tenderness. She swells beneath his touch. He strokes her body with firm assurance. He licks her breasts, sucks her nipples and parts her thighs with a confidence that borders on boldness. She knows he has done this before, but she doesn't ask and he doesn't tell. When he slides his fingers inside her she gasps with pleasure and opens her eyes to his smiling face. She pulls him into her and shudders with him. He envelops her and grunts in response to her loud moans. Their limbs remain tangled and slick as they fall asleep on top of the covers.

They read the papers and go for walks. She runs through piles of leaves and throws handfuls of them into the sky. He warns her to watch out for dog mess. She cooks him dinner. They don't have many pans so she can't make meat and two veg. She experiments, sometimes successfully. She makes chilli with too much cayenne pepper; she puts salt in the apple crumble; her baking never rises. She blames the different ingredients. She discovers bologna and makes it into everything from casseroles to stir-fry. He eats whatever she puts before him and pretends to enjoy it.

They build snowmen and have snowball fights. Her aim is surprisingly good. He teaches her to make snow angels by lying on her back and waving her arms up and down in the snow. She loves the impressions they make lying side by side. He builds her a toboggan and pulls her to the top of hills. They fly down together and end up clutching each other in a giggling heap at the bottom. They drink mugs of hot chocolate to warm up. She makes it with milk. He adds a tot of rum.

They get married. It is a small ceremony at a hotel. She would have liked to invite her sister and her mother, but he wants to do it straight away and likes the secrecy and immediacy. Their witnesses are strangers. Jean wears a white mini-dress and knee-high boots. He asks her to leave them on when they get to their room. She slips from the bed and his gently snoring body and stands naked on the balcony. Her nipples stiffen in the cold and she wraps her arms around her body. She looks down at the headlights of the cars as they race by in the night.

Jean thinks of the things she doesn't know about him: his favourite colour; his shoe size; where he would most like to travel; how many children he wants; his family; his past.

Jean tells him she is pregnant. She hopes he will be happy. He isn't. He shouts and becomes ugly. She only hears some of what he says. He says 'extra mouth to feed', he says 'overseas placement', he says 'ruin my career', he says 'abortion', he says 'stupid bitch', he says 'divorce'.

4

Jean sighs as she looks out of the window. The view hasn't changed for hours now. She sees endless plains of grass. She knows why they are called plains; there are no distinguishing features or points of interest. The wind whirls through the grass and it looks alive, but the beasts that lurk within never materialise.

The woman seated beside her hands her an apple. The woman has long grey hair parted in the middle and gathered into two plaits which fall over her shoulders and spill down her front. Throughout the journey she has been reaching into a bag at her feet and pulling out treasures which she shares silently with Jean. She doesn't ask if Jean wants the apple, the tomato, the boiled egg, she just passes them to her and Jean, not wanting to cause offence and actually quite hungry, smiles and accepts.

Jean smoothes her hands over her skirt. The woman sees her do this. She sees the way her hands caress her stomach and she guesses. Jean twists the ring on her finger. She has a wedding ring and a baby on the way, but she doesn't know if she has a husband. The woman pats her hand and smiles at Jean. Somehow she is comforted by this gesture from a stranger and she falls asleep.

Mornington Crescent

****

Jean is jolted awake. She was dreaming of wild Indians. She knows that Henry is from the Lakota tribe. He told her this when she pressed him. He won't talk about it any more. She is coming to see his people. He would probably laugh at that. She doesn't know why she is coming or what she expects to find, but she knows nothing about them and their blood is mixed now. She tried to learn about their ways, but her head is full of names and Hollywood images.

Red Cloud, Sitting Bull, Rain in the Face, Little Crow, Standing Bear, Crazy Horse; she has heard the names. She has seen films of war-whooping Indians on horseback with bows and arrows and eagle feather headdresses, attacking wagon trains and scalping innocent passengers. She is a little afraid.

She hears a low steady rumble and she knows it is this that has awakened her. Outside the windows, all is dark, but she feels the endless plains are still there, stretching to the horizon like an ocean of possibilities, rippling on the surface with suggestion. The noise increases and the bus shudders. She glances at the old woman who is serene.

'Used to be, it was either a storm or a herd of buffalo approaching. Sure ain't no buffalo now.'

Jean listens to the thunder swell and crash against the vast caverns of the sky. The echoes roll back to her and she imagines the thundering hooves of a wild stampede. A fork of lightning briefly illuminates the plains and the lights flicker. Seconds later a deafening peal of thunder sounds directly overhead. The passengers gasp and whimper, and the bus is charged with trepidation.

The woman beside her takes out a bread roll which she breaks and passes half to Jean. Calmly she pops a piece into her mouth and Jean watches as she chews. She is not concerned. Jean wonders what it would be like to face the extremes of the elements from within a cone of rawhide. There is nothing to fear.

****

Jean is on another bus. She is heading from Pierre to Pine Ridge. The old woman has gone. The other passengers have sullen stoic faces. They don't look at her but she knows they have seen her. She is too bright and shiny here. Her red hair and pale face are out of place.

The bus is full so she stands and sways with the motion. She feels nauseous and would love a drink of water. As the bus stops abruptly she staggers and nearly falls. Brown hands reach out to steady her. They are adorned with bracelets of shells and beads. She looks around to say thank you but no one is looking at her. Their gestures are instinctive; they would not let someone fall in their presence. She mumbles her thanks to the bus in general and she sees a man nod slightly. His eyes remain fixed straight ahead.

****

People have drifted away. There are shouts as they are met and greeted and taken elsewhere. Jean stands with her bag at her feet in the dust. She looks at the wooden cabins with something like anger. This is the land of the free and the home of the brave. How can there be such poverty? There are flies and smells and darkness. There is no running water, electricity or sanitation. Children are playing a game of chase and their bare feet and ragged laughter fly past her.

She stands there a long time, immobile. Is this why Henry never talked about his past? Was he ashamed? Or did he think she would be? Tears spring to her eyes as she feels for him. She would never think less of him for his background. She is proud of him.

A woman approaches, shuffling in beaded moccasins and holding a bawling infant. Jean instinctively places her hand on her stomach.

'Are you waiting for somebody?'

'No, I, um, I don't know anybody.'

The woman nods as though this is perfectly normal behaviour. She shifts the infant to her other hip and flicks her long black braid out of its clutches. Jean sees that she is really just a young girl.

'Come and eat with us.'

Jean can neither accept nor decline before the girl has turned and began walking towards a shack from which shouts and laughter are emanating. She realises that maybe it was more of a command than an invitation. She picks up her bag and follows, ducking through the doorway. The noises stop as she enters and her eyes take a few seconds to adjust to the gloom.

The girl places the baby in a wooden cradle and gives it a rag to suck on. Amazingly, it becomes quiet. There are seven other people in the room; an older man and two older women, plus a range of boys and girls with black hair and dark eyes. They all look at her, but she doesn't feel threatened. The girl who came over to her gestures towards a seat.

'She has nowhere to go. She needs food.'

They all begin moving again, pulling up chairs and urging her to sit down. The older woman goes to a steaming pot and ladles out a sort of stew onto chipped plates which are passed around. Jean has no idea what it is, but she eats hungrily. No one talks as they scrape up every last bit of food and then pass around mugs of something dark and strong and slightly bitter. Jean notices the men take theirs outside and the women pull their chairs into a circle. They look at her expectantly.

'My name is Jean. I'm from England. My husband, Henry Waters, is from here, I think. He is Lakota.'

She blushes and stumbles over her words. She is not sure what she should say or whether she is pronouncing it correctly. She senses that she could easily offend without meaning to. She doesn't want to upset these people who have been so kind without question and shared with her although they have next to nothing. The girl picks up the baby and fastens it to her breast. Jean yearns to hold it. The old woman nods, and she continues.

'He didn't tell me anything about his background or his family. Now he's left and I'm not sure if he's coming back. I don't know where he is. I think this is his home. He may have come back here?'

Even as she says this, Jean knows that he hasn't; that he has never set foot here since the day he left. They know it too. The woman's soft gaze urges her on.

'I thought if I knew something about who he is, where he came from, I might be able to understand him.

Maybe someone might know him? Actually, I don't know why I came here. I just couldn't go back to England, not like this, not without him. I don't want them to know I've failed. I tried so hard to do something by myself, something good, but it looks like I can't even do that.'

Jean realises she is crying again. The women let her. She mumbles things about being silly and being sorry, thanking them for their hospitality and the food and kindness. She tries not to mention the conditions. She doesn't know what she says. She realises none of them have said anything and she grinds to a halt. The old woman stands.

'You will stay here tonight. Then you will go back to your people. They will look after you and the baby.'

Once again, there is no argument or discussion. Jean is shown through to the other room of the cabin where there are rugs and blankets piled on the wooden floor. She sees that the whole family and perhaps others sleep in here. She thinks she can't possibly sleep in a room full of strangers, but they indicate that she must lie down and she doesn't want to offend anyone. The girl with the baby unfurls a mat close to the wall and smiles at Jean.

'I am Rising Dawn. I will sleep here beside you. You are safe.'

And Jean knows that she is safe. She is also very tired, and as she lies down and closes her eyes, she falls asleep almost at once.

****

Jean sleeps deeply and doesn't hear the others come to bed. She wakes once in the middle of the night and sees that the room is full of wrapped bodies which stir and mutter softly. In the moonlight she sees Rising Dawn suckling her baby, looking peaceful and content. The girl sees her awake and smiles. She takes something from around her neck and holds it out to Jean. As Jean reaches out to take it she sees it is a beaded image of a turtle on a leather thong. The girl presses it into her hand and whispers,

'You will have a healthy baby girl.'

The sound of heavy breathing all around is comforting. As Jean falls asleep again, she realises that she never mentioned there was going to be a baby.

5

Jean takes the money. There is so much of it. She has not got used to American money; it's all the same colour and sometimes she finds it difficult to tell which notes are which, but she can tell there is a lot here. It makes her nervous. The teller raises her eyebrows and Jean steps away from the counter.

'Next please.'

The queue shuffles forwards and Jean pushes the money into her shoulder bag. She has been told to always carry this in front, where she can see it, and to keep her eye, and preferably hand, on it at all times. It feels red hot and she wants to take it out and check it, but that is silly; she only just put it in there and it can't have gone anywhere.

Outside she realises that she is hungry. She hasn't eaten all day and the smells from the food stalls are appealing. She would love one of those artificial hotdogs kennelled in the bland bun with the red sauce and the mustard that doesn't taste of anything. As she salivates, she knows it is only the onions that excite her with their caramel hue and bitter-sweet aroma.

Maybe later; she is on a mission. She smiles; it has been too long since she felt she had a purpose, and this is the most definite plan she has made since she came here in the first place. Her pace quickens as she crosses the street. She is smiling at everybody until she thinks that this may draw attention to herself and she looks down at her sensible shoes as they flash along the pavement or sidewalk as they call it.

Skipping down to the underpass, she wrinkles her nose at the tang of urine. Well, that has certainly taken her appetite away. Her stomach lurches and she puts her hand to it to calm it down. She sees two young men walking towards her. She assumes they are young men, but she can't tell their age because they are both wearing hats pulled low and scarves pulled high so that hardly any of their face is showing. She notices that it is quiet down here and cold, although she finds herself sweating. There is no one else around and she suddenly feels afraid and threatened, but she is too far into the tunnel to turn and run, and they would run faster than her anyway. She tells herself she is being dramatic and alarmist and she carries on, keeping her focus dead ahead and gripping her bag.

The two men pass close by her, one on either side. She is careful not to look at them and they don't say anything. She lets out her breath with relief but won't look back. She imagines a pillar of salt like the woman turned into in one of Claire's stories. She can taste the salt in the blood on her lip which she has bitten in her anxiety. All will be well now and she will be safe.

The hand on her shoulder spins her around and she is staring into the man's eyes. They are blue, she notices. She has never liked blue eyes. Heroines in novels indicate their goodness with the blueness of their eyes which is matched only by the fairness of their hair and the blandness of their character. All babies have blue eyes until they form individual personalities. She has always seen them as deceitful as though they have something to hide. These ones stare at her, and although the man still says nothing, she sees his intentions clearly enough. His hand is at her throat as he pushes her against the wall. She tries to cough but he is pressing into her. She feels his thumb on her throat, his knee jammed against her thigh, and what the hell is that?

She strains to look down and she sees the metal barrel prodding in her belly; its sleek ridges are obscene against the gentle swell of her body. She is furious. She yells in anger, she raises her fist and strikes the man on the side of the head. He is stunned and backs away, shaking his head in confusion or possibly pain. The other man grabs her bag and tries to pull it from her shoulder. She shrugs as though to free it and then holding it with both hands she beats him, screaming and snarling. He looks scared. He should be. She is going to have this baby in England; how dare they try and stop her?

Her screams echo in the cavernous passage as she runs. The men don't follow her this time. She runs all the way to the travel agent and pushes through the door into their calm and ordered world. The assistant looks up, startled as she sinks into a chair.

'Can I help you?' he asks in a tone that suggests he really rather wouldn't.

Jean takes the money from her purse and his eyes widen as she sees the value of the notes. She pushes them across the counter to him.

'Get me a passage to England. I want to go home.'

'Of course, Miss.'

He bustles about screening his discomfort with efficiency and manners, and twenty minutes later she has a receipt for a ticket which will come shortly and allow her to travel. He coughs discreetly and suggests that some companies don't like it when women travel when they're pregnant.

'How interesting' she replies. She will tell them she is fat.

She has very little change from the transaction, but she folds it away in her purse. It looks a little battered. When she stands to leave, her legs are very weak and she isn't sure if she can make it to the door. She feels cold and damp and is horrified. What if her waters have broken and she's losing the baby? Or having it here after she's just spent all her money on a boat ticket? She is relieved to discover she has merely wet herself and the knowledge is enough to carry her out. The assistant isn't nearly so pleased.

6

Paddington

Zone 1: Bakerloo (between Warwick Avenue and Edgware Road); Circle and District (between Bayswater and Edgware Road); Hammersmith and City (between Royal Oak and Edgware Road). Connections with National Rail.

Nearby attractions: Albert Memorial; Kensington Gardens; Little Venice; Serpentine Gallery.

Paddington Station, also known as London Paddington (but not by Londoners who simply call it Paddington), was the original Western terminus for the world's first underground railway.

The mainline station was designed by Isambard Kingdom Brunel and it is here that Michael Bond chose to abandon his fictional bear from Deepest Darkest Peru. In deference to the childhood evacuees who passed through here, the bear was found with merely a battered suitcase and a luggage tag around his neck requesting someone to 'Please look after this bear. Thank you.' He was taken in by the Brown family who did indeed look after him.

Clearly the bear was far luckier than the male child found at the station in 1961. His decomposing body was found stuffed into a suitcase with paper stuffed into his mouth, and his identity was never discovered. Agatha

Christie also used the station as the starting point for one of her murder mysteries: '4.50 from Paddington'.

Just north of Paddington Station is the confluence of the Grand Union Canal and the Regent's Canal, known as Little Venice. The desirable residential area is known for its pubs, cafes, shops and theatres, and is home to the BBC Maida Vale studios. It is a prime setting for stories and secrets.

****

Jean has a long time to think on the journey. She doesn't need to think; she knows what she wants to do. It is so simple. She wants to go home: she wants to have her baby. There will be time enough then to worry about what to do next. All will be well. She doesn't know how, but she knows it will be. Claire will meet her and look after her for a while and she doesn't need to think.

People around her are sick and ill. They say the rolling motion makes their stomach heave. Jean loves the salty spray on her lips. She watches the white foam trail that the propeller leaves behind. She imagines it churning through all the misery and heartache and making the world clean and fresh. People say they are bored with nothing to do. Jean loves the meals in the dining room and the orchestra playing.

She sits or walks or stands on deck. She scans the empty horizon, full of possibility and nothingness. She crochets a blanket. She has a pattern of a giraffe, but she runs out of yellow wool and it ends up with stumpy legs. It might not be able to reach the highest branches, but it can drink from the deepest pools.

Mornington Crescent

****

Claire meets her from the ship, with a baby in her arms.

'Meet Jennifer, your new niece.'

She gurgles and smiles at Jean, reaching out tiny hands to the blanket she carries, taking it for herself without asking for permission. Jean shrugs and laughs. She can't deny the child anything. She is so pleased to be here.

Claire takes her home. James answers the door with his wild hair trying to escape from his head and the calm expression in his eyes. There is chaos inside and Claire sighs as she picks her way through toys and toddlers.

'Everything alright, darling?'

'What? Hmm, yes, bit of a problem with this particular equation, but I've just had an idea.'

He retreats to the study to thrash out his latest solution. Jean stands transfixed in the doorway as Claire wades through to the kitchen and puts the kettle on. The baby wakes up and begins crying. Jean lugs her own bags inside, putting them down amidst drying sheets and socks hung over the backs of chairs. There is so much movement that she doesn't know where to stand without feeling in the way.

Claire switches into instant mummy mode. She cuddles Ruth and helps her dress her doll, stops Adam throwing the football at Emma, suggesting he take it outside instead, admires Emma's imaginary tea party she has laid out for her teddy bears, and prepares beans on toast for them all. She gives Jean a cup of tea and runs her a bath. She shows her the tiny room with the freshly made bed and the clean towels. She says she will have dinner ready for her soon. She shoos Jean out of her way and takes her bags upstairs.

Jean is amazed. She is overwhelmed. She is home.

****

The children go to nursery school. The baby sleeps and feeds. Jean rests and drinks tea. The days go by.

Claire washes and cleans and cooks and dusts and shops and Jean thinks that nothing has changed, except that now Claire has more people to look after. She wonders why Claire left and went to study when she is back where she started.

They take a train to see their mother. Joyce is busy but happy to see them. She has made eggy custard especially. Jean hates eggy custard and wonders why she thinks it is her favourite, but she eats it and doesn't correct her. Joyce has moved into a small flat and still writes, but her stories are no longer accepted. Times and readers have changed. She tells them that she can spare a couple of hours, but then she has to 'get back to it'.

She asks after James and the children. She checks that Jean is well and healthy and listens to her stories from America. She says she has always wanted to travel. She likes the sound of New Zealand. Jean thinks the idea of her mother travelling is quite ludicrous. She can't imagine her straying far from her desk. She wonders what she knows about New Zealand, or whether its appeal lies in its distance and anonymity.

Joyce doesn't ask about Henry. No one does. On the train on the way home, Jean watches the fields flash by and she twists her wedding ring on her finger.

'I think she's losing her mind.'

Jean is shocked. She looks at Claire who is rocking Jennifer.

'Who, mum?'

Who else? But Jean wants to be sure. Claire nods sadly. The silence is broken only by the clacking of the wheels. Jean can't think of what to say. She wants to deny it, but what does she know? She hasn't been here, and Claire should know; Claire always knows.

'What makes you say that?'

'She repeats things. She forgets what time of day it is and what she had for breakfast. She doesn't know how old I am, or what my children are called. She hasn't written a book for quite a while. She keeps starting them, but never finishing them.'

'But, she could just be getting forgetful. She's getting old.'

Claire smiles and shakes her head gently.

'She's only fifty-one.'

The baby is asleep. Jean holds out her arms and Claire carefully hands her over. Jean hugs the warm bundle to her breast. She feels the life and the fragility. She remembers how Joyce held her so tightly on the day of the bomb and promised to look after her and keep her safe. What if she can't anymore? Who is going to look after whom? A tear falls on Jennifer's forehead and Jean wipes it away. Claire gets up to go to the toilet; to allow this news to sink in; to give her space. Jean looks out of the window again and listens to the rhythm of the train.

Losing her mind. Losing her mind. Losing her mind.

7

Elephant and Castle

Zone 1: Bakerloo (terminus – previous stop is Lambeth North); Northern (between Kennington and Borough). Connections with National Rail.

Nearby Attractions: The Cinema Museum; The Imperial War Museum; The Cuming Museum.

At the evocatively-named Elephant and Castle, you will not find an elephant, or a castle, but a roundabout at a central London major road intersection, and a shopping centre.

You will find the Michael Faraday Memorial; a stainless-steel box intended to commemorate the great Victorian scientist and pioneer of electromagnetism. The designer had intended the casing of the structure to be glass, allowing the internal workings of the transformer to be seen, but the fear of vandalism prevented this. With its steel casing and lack of obvious connection to Faraday (or, indeed, anyone), many people have no idea what it is or why it is there.

The name comes from an inn which occupied the site from the 1700s. One of the tales of how this inn got its name is that Eleanor of Castille, the Spanish Infanta, stopped here en route to meeting her future husband, Charles I. As her title was La Infanta de Castille, a theory is that this was mangled by the English tongue into the semantically random pairing of Elephant and Castle.

The first baby born on the London Underground came into the world at this station in 1924. Press reports claimed that she had been named Thelma Ursula Beatrice Eleanor, so that her initials would spell out TUBE. Unfortunately, like most good stories, this proved to be untrue, and she was actually called Marie Cordery.

****

'I'm so scared.'

Jean is drenched in sweat. Her sister holds her hand and looks directly into her eyes.

'It's okay. It will be okay. You're doing so well.'

Claire has been through this before. She knows it will be okay. But she also knows how frightening it can be, and she had a husband by her side.

Jean is so tired. She hates the contractions that rip through her. She will never have another baby. She wants to scream, and curse, but everyone here is being so helpful. She stores her vitriol for those who are absent. She has been at this for hours; writhing and contorting. People say that giving birth is the most natural thing in the world. Another spasm racks her body. How can this be natural? Women used to die in childbirth and it was called survival of the fittest. She doesn't feel very fit. In the old days, she would have been sacrificed to evolution. She doesn't even know whether she wants this little parasite inside her. This is all too hard. She just wants it to stop.

'I *am* sodding pushing!'

She can't breathe. Tears and snot run into her mouth. It's so unglamorous. No one told her it would be like this. No one talks about this agony. If they did, perhaps the population would dwindle to nothing. It's all a massive conspiracy and she has been duped. This is exquisite torture and she would tell anyone anything they wanted to know.

'Just ask me', she thinks, 'I'd rather have my toenails pulled out one by one'.

Claire is so calm, she wants to slap her. She is a saint. It can't have been like this for her. She must have had it easy, or how can she sit there like that, looking so supportive and so bloody encouraging?

'It hurts!'

No one seems to understand. She needs to tell them, to wipe those smug smiles off their face. The nurses nod primly like they've seen it all before. Well, she hasn't and they need to know what she's going through.

Apparently the head is coming. Someone is fiddling about between her legs and they are telling her that everything is okay. Well they should be in her position. Lying here with her legs in stirrups and her insides falling out, everything is far from sodding okay.

'I can't.'

She looks up at Claire, pleading. She can make it stop, just as she always has. She has been smiling softly and nodding sympathetically, she can make everything okay, just as she has promised it will be.

'Alright, well, I'll just ask them to put it back.'

Jean gasps, 'No way!'"

She grips Claire's hand tightly, but Claire doesn't even wince.

'I have to' she pants aloud and Claire nods. Yes, she does. The nurses ask Claire to leave and Jean's eye's fill with panic.

'I'll be right here,' Claire soothes. She steps back out of the delivery room and watches through the glass partition as Jean wrestles with the force of life. Amid the sterile cloths and the steel machinery her sister looks abducted. She looks alone.

****

It's a healthy baby girl. Claire looks at her lying in a cradle with a small band around her wrist. Baby Waters. Her face is screwed up tightly in sleep. She will be tired after all that bawling. There is certainly no trouble with her lungs, as she let the world know from the start how indignant she was with it. She will be the boss, Claire thinks as she strokes the glass, wishing she could feel the soft olive skin and the mass of hair beneath her fingers. She will break hearts.

Baby Waters is born with a full head of hair. As the nurse cleans and swaddles the baby, crooning to Jean that she is perfect and beautiful, Jean struggles to sit and demands,

'What colour?'

When she hears about the damp jet-black tresses, she smiles and subsides.

'Thank God it isn't red.'

Jean sleeps in another room. Claire drinks hideous hospital coffee from a paper cup which leaks and drips. There is a waiting room but it is full of nerves and twitches. She wants to be calm. She wants a moment before she returns to her family with their cries and needs and mountains of washing. She tears herself away from the window and sees a man standing awkwardly with a bunch of flowers twisted in his giant hands. His eyes scan the rows of cots until they alight on the one he wants. His tough features soften. He looks unused to confusion. Claire watches as he runs his hand through his black, black hair and she knows.

'Henry?'

He nods. She waits but he says nothing, merely looking down at his feet. She takes this as an indication of shame and some of her anger dissipates. So he should be ashamed. He has treated her sister terribly and left her to pick up the pieces. But he is here now, and she knows that he doesn't need recriminations.

'I'm Claire.'

He nods again. She is struck by his silence. More than just unease, she feels that words are redundant to this colossus of a man. She holds out her hand to shake his and he takes it, swallowing it in his palm. She doesn't usually shake hands with people and she doesn't know what to do when he doesn't let go.

'Jean's through here.'

She leads him like a child down a white corridor past squeaking shoes and starched uniforms to a small ward which contains their happiness. He finally drops her hand as he falls to his knees by the side of Jean's bed and rests his head upon the blanket. Claire stands in the doorway, unsure if she should witness the reunion, but worried that her sister might need her. She is so fragile and vulnerable right now. Jean stirs and opens her eyes. She turns her head and smiles into his eyes. There is no surprise on her face, just radiant warmth.

Mornington Crescent

'Hey there Hal,' she whispers. 'We've got a beautiful baby daughter.'

'I saw her,' he whispers back.

'I'm sorry. I'm so sorry.'

Jean holds out her arms to his shuddering body. Claire watches her frail little sister tell him,

'It's okay. It will be okay.'

He mumbles so that Claire can barely hear. 'I love you.'

'I love you too.'

All the necessary words have been said. Claire leaves the room and walks back down the lonely corridor wiping away traces of tears.

8

Victoria

Zone 1: Circle (between Sloane Square and St James' Park); District (between Sloane Square and St James' Park); Victoria (between Pimlico and Green Park). Connections with National Rail.

Nearby attractions: Buckingham Palace; St James' Park; Westminster Cathedral.

London Victoria is the second busiest underground station in London (after Waterloo) with eight million passengers passing through annually. First opened in 1868 it was not designed for this level of traffic and severe congestion necessitates crowd control measures. At busy times entrances are closed, with only the exits open until the overcrowding is relieved. This can last from a couple of minutes to several hours and travellers are often advised to avoid the station altogether.

Nearby Buckingham Palace was originally built in 1705 for the Duke of Buckingham (it was called Buckingham House) and did not become the official royal palace until 1837 when Queen Victoria moved in. There were several design faults including poor heating, lighting and ventilation – it was cold, dark and smelly. When Victoria married Albert in 1840 he set himself the task of fixing these problems.

King George VI and Queen Elizabeth famously refused to leave the palace during World War II, thereby winning the affection of the people across the country. The Queen toured the devastated areas of London to show solidarity with fellow residents and reflected, "The people are marvellous and full of fight. One could not imagine that life could become so terrible. We must win in the end." The palace was bombed seven times while the reigning monarch was in residence, and the chapel was completely destroyed. She said, "I'm glad we have been bombed. Now we can look the East End in the face."

On the day of the Battle of Britain, RAF fighter pilot Sergeant Ray 'Arty' Holmes, while flying in a Hurricane, saw a German bomber he believed was on course to bomb Buckingham Palace. He had run out of ammunition so his guns wouldn't operate and instead he chose to ram the bomber and take its tailplane off with his wing. The bomber crashed into the forecourt of Victoria Station and Holmes bailed out of his plane which hit the ground at 350mph and was buried beneath a watermain. The site on Buckingham Palace Road was since paved over.

Holmes' parachute caught on a drainpipe and he claims, "I ended up dangling just off the ground with my feet in a dustbin." Having identified himself he was hailed as a hero by the local residents and treated to several brandies at the Orange Brewery before being returned to his squadron in a taxi.

In 2004 archaeologist Christopher Bennett led an excavation team to cordon off one of London's busiest junctions between Buckingham Palace and Victoria Station to see what remained of the plane. The team recovered the engine, sections of the wooden tail fin, the fuselage and a section of hydraulic pipe. These pieces are now in London's Imperial War Museum.

****

Jean and Henry stay indefinitely. The eldest children are at school learning alphabets and numbers. With a teacher for a mother, they can already read and write and they learn superiority and intellectual privilege early. Emma trails behind the twins, Ruth and Adam. They are in different classes but still seem to be always together.

Henry gets work building things; mainly houses and extensions. Families are everywhere and children spring up like daisies. Claire and Jean push the prams to the park and watch the toddlers on the see saws. They plonk their babies on the grass with fistfuls of stale bread. They encourage them to throw it to the ducks and Jennifer does, evenly distributing it, but Dawn clings to hers until the ducks come to peck it out of her tiny mitts and she wails.

James goes to work in the city. He wears a suit and tie, but he doesn't polish his shoes or comb his hair. He is developing business machines which are the future. He tells Emma that he sells cabbages, which is how he sneeringly thinks of these monstrous machines. She envisages him pushing a barrow through the streets of London laden with fresh groceries.

In the evenings, after the children are in bed, James and Henry listen to cricket coverage on the wireless and James explains the interminable rules. Henry gets bamboozled by silly mid-ons and he stalks outside with his pipe, taking a turn around the square. He studies books and almanacs but still can't understand the enigmatic language. Often they play chess in games which take hours and employ underhand tactics as they seek to topple the crown. They discuss opening gambits and endgames as they lean back in their chairs to survey the aerial battlefield. Claire hates to see the pyre of wooden pieces as they pile up in a morgue of casualty.

Claire thinks it is a cruel game and she and Jean sit at the kitchen table with a glass of cheap wine each. They embroider tapestries which they frame and hang on the wall or take to their mother, who loses them. How can you lose a three foot square canvas? She just doesn't remember where she's put them. They work on a picture of a cornucopia, spilling forth riches. The sheaves of corn and ripe fruits are made of bright tiny beads and Claire keeps them all in separate boxes according to colour. She methodically covers the squares of the canvas in sequence, whereas Jean completes the images she likes: a vibrant orange pumpkin here; a brilliant green gourd there.

It is the same with jigsaw puzzles. Claire hunts through the pieces to find the corners and then forms the edges and continues inwards. She likes the order and turns all the pieces over on a board, grouping them in specific clusters. Jean configures the people and animals or any writing. She gets bored with sky, mountains and pastures and trails her fingers through a jumbled kaleidoscope of Swiss alpine scenery. James wanders into the kitchen looking for leftover custard and won't leave until he taps a piece triumphantly into place. Jean always hides a random shape at the beginning so that she can be the one to complete the picture. They all stand around and admire the large reproduction of the image on the box and then they break it into fragments and put it back.

****

They are all huddled around the television set. Valerie has the only one in the square and she has invited them all round. Usually they wouldn't have gone to Valerie's house for her to show off her ornaments and accoutrements. She is collectively condemned by the way she puts the milk bottle directly on to the table and eschews a milk jug. There are a myriad of other manners the young mothers sniff at, but they are here today. They will not cut off their nose to spite their face. What else would they look down?

The curtains are drawn against the daylight, although there is no sun. The sky is grey and a light drizzle falls. Some of the older children are playing outside on the green, but the younger ones are clasped on laps. Wriggling and bawling is not allowed, as history is being made in the corner of the room, flickering in black and white images between walnut doors.

Jean watches the eight white horses pulling the golden coach. She has been told it is a golden coach, but it looks grey. The horses, borrowed from Cinderella along with the footmen, are clearly white. The streets leading to the Abbey are lined with people who stand waving and cheering behind lines of men with sombre uniforms and sabres and funny white hats. Jean feels terribly proud to be British. We can crown queens, win cricket and conquer mountains. Dawn is asleep in her arms. She glances at Claire, wondering whether to be guilty that her daughter has slid into disrespectful slumber.

Claire stands still with wide eyes fixed on the 9-inch screen. She cradles Jennifer on her hip and the little girl reaches out chubby hands to the coaches of dignitaries

Mornington Crescent

and royalty. Winston Churchill glides by. People have whispered that Winston is a little bit in love with the young queen, and why wouldn't he be? In her open-top carriage despite the rain, the Queen of Tonga is fabulous and flamboyant, and Claire frowns. She may be showing deference, but Claire thinks she is showing off.

Richard Dimbleby's voice rolls out of the television set in plums of reverential awe, as he describes the scene inside the Abbey. As the Queen walks up to her throne, Claire thinks of her wedding and how this aisle can feel like a gauntlet. Faces turn to stare with smiles and tears of emotion. Claire had her husband to greet her at the end of the tunnel. Elizabeth has an empty throne and a lot of old serious looking men. Claire aches with pity for this young lady who will be her queen.

Jean studies her dress with a critical eye. It is almost a bridal gown of white silk and cream taffeta, but it is nothing like what Jean wore when she wed Henry. There are flowers and symbols of all the Commonwealth countries woven into the fabric with silk, crystals, jewels and pearls. She imagines stitching the soft green fern of New Zealand at her sister's table. She giggles to think of this most powerful woman covered in leeks, thistles and leaves. Six maids struggle along behind carrying her velvet robe. Richard Dimbleby recites its origins and its importance. It looks heavy.

It grows warm in the stuffy drawing room. Jean stifles a yawn as orbs, sceptres, rods and rings are bandied about. Apparently the ritual goes back 1,200 years. Jean feels as though it is taking that long. She wants to shuffle and fidget, but nobody stirs as the Archbishop of Canterbury pours oil over the Queen's forehead, and places the striking crown upon her curls. Claire smiles at Jean, remembering how she could never keep her school beret on her curls and Jean grins back, thinking exactly the same thing. Her beret didn't weigh nearly as much or wink diamonds. She is impressed with the Queen's poise and balance.

Claire realises that Elizabeth is about the same age as Jean and she feels a surge of affection for her as she says in a small, calm voice,

'The things which I have here before promised, I will perform and keep. So help me God. Throughout my life and with all my heart I shall strive to be worthy of your trust.'

She is small but strong as the shouts ring out, 'God save Queen Elizabeth.' As everybody stands to toast the new queen and Valerie passes around the sherry, Jean notices there are tears running down Claire's cheeks. The smell instantly takes Claire back to her father's funeral and she feels sick. Jean is at her side and she hurries her out to the square where Union Jack bunting flaps in the breeze. The rain has stopped and the sky begins to clear. Claire gulps down lungfuls of fresh air scented with mown grass, cut especially for today.

Ruth cannons into her stomach. She wants to know if they can have lemonade. There is a stall set up under one of the trees and tumblers with paper straws are being handed out to all the children. Claire says yes they can, just this once, and she watches as the unaccustomed sugar careens through them. They swing on tree branches and practice gymnastics. Ruth and Emma leap into Arab springs and Adam walks on his hands.

Claire thanks Valerie and watches as their children play together. Valerie's daughters have special coronation mugs which they let the others drink from. Jennifer squirms on her mother's hip and Claire puts her down on the grass. She sees the girls playing tea parties and she begins a determined crawl towards them. Crawling isn't fast enough and soon she is on her feet, tottering her first steps. Claire claps her hands and laughs. Everyone in the square shares the precious moment. They are all one family today.

James organises a spontaneous game of cricket – six and you're out, even the children. The little ones each get a go at bat although they don't have to field. Sausage rolls and sponge cakes appear from various kitchens and it isn't even a competition. Henry whips off his jumper and forms goalposts for football. He understands this sport a lot better than cricket. Valerie's husband, Bill, sets up the wireless outside and they dance to big band sounds in the square. Children stay up way past their bedtime, high on lemonade and a sense of occasion. They run onto the makeshift dance floor and tangle up in the legs of the adults. Henry holds Jean close as he steps inside the lyrics and whispers them in her hair,

'Stars shining bright above you,
Night breezes seem to whisper, I love you.'

Some parents tuck their children into bed and drift back to the square where they sway and laugh. Other children, not wanting to miss the magic of this special day, slump on benches or curl under trees. James touches Claire's hand and she smiles up at him as the music swirls around them. She thinks how lucky she is to be here and now. America may have Frankie Laine, Perry Como, Patti Page and Johnnie Ray, but they have a family and Queen Elizabeth II.

9

Regent's Park

Zone 1: Bakerloo (between Baker Street and Oxford Circus).
Nearby attractions: London Zoo; Madame Tussauds; Regent's Park.

Regent's Park is one of the Royal Parks of London and covers 197 acres including Primrose Hill and comprises an open air theatre, London Zoo and public recreation and leisure facilities. During the Dissolution of the Monasteries, Henry VIII appropriated Regent's Park in 1538 as a hunting ground, considering it to be an invigorating ride from Whitehall.

The park remained largely unchanged until after the Civil War. Between 1649 and 1666 the Commonwealth government (under Oliver Cromwell) chopped down many trees to repay the country's war debts. In 1811 the Prince Regent (later George IV) wanted a summer palace, so his friend and architect to the crown, John Nash designed the style of the park we know today. He also planned a royal residence, but the Prince turned his attention to improving Buckingham Palace instead.

Not until 1835 (during the reign of King William IV) were the general public allowed into some sections, two days a week, for carriage rides. Now there are puppet shows, picnic areas, deck chairs, cafes, running routes, floodlit courts at the tennis centre, boat hire at the Boat House, and various activities at The Hub where punters can play cricket, football, boules, softball and rugby on the pitches – although not all at the same time, so booking is necessary.

Exotic animals abound at London Zoo, within the park. Here you can see penguins, pelicans, and otters; lions, tigers, and monkeys; gorillas, giraffes, and merekats; sloths, armadillos, and crocodiles; Galapagos tortoises, pygmy hippos, and komodo dragons; emu, flamingos, and vultures.

****

It is Boxing Day and so they will go for a walk. It is what they do on Boxing Day; never mind that it is freezing, that the river has flooded and there is treacherous ice everywhere. Joyce has laced up her sturdy walking boots and she is champing at the bit, anxious to get to the pub for her Christmas sherry. James and Henry have already left the house, walking with hands clasped behind their back, deep in serious conversation about reinforced concrete and design principles.

Claire and Jean do battle with the children; doling out scarves and hats and mittens, certain that the same number won't return from the excursion. Claire has a thermos of hot blackcurrant and spare sets of clothing in a backpack, which she will lug around with her. She has got some homemade chocolate shortbread in case of emergencies and some money to buy crisps at the pub as the children will sit outside on the porch fighting over cheese and onion or prawn cocktail. She has tried getting all ready-salted to put a stop to the arguments, but this is apparently boring.

The children race out of the house and clatter off down the alleyway towards the field and the river. Claire panics; will James stop them all from falling in and drowning themselves? Has she left the oven at the correct temperature so that the ham will be ready when they get back? She'd best pop back and check. There is also the slow cooker on the stovetop full of bones and skin and tight brown onions slowly changing yesterday's turkey carcass into tomorrow's soup and next month's stock.

Jennifer and Dawn are not as eager as the rest. It was warm indoors with books and puzzles. It is cold out and the trees are bare of leaves and berries; there is nothing to look at. Even the squirrels are hibernating and the forlorn ducks have nothing to swim on. They waddle over the ice; their webbed feet sliding and dumping them ignominiously on their feathery bellies. Dawn lags behind and whines. Jean is stern for once, she knows the brisk walk will do them good, and she doesn't want to let the side down.

Claire brings up the rear. She feels military, buttoned into her coat with responsibility like martial pips on her shoulders. Isn't it curious how martial is an anagram of marital?

'Come on Claire! James calls from up front. 'What are you playing at?' He has obviously been told to wait for her and is irritated at the interruption. Claire sighs and starts to jog to catch up. She hates running. Everything wobbles inappropriately and it doesn't help when James says,

'Look at mummy running. Doesn't she look silly?' and all the children laugh. She smiles wanly to show that of course she has a sense of humour, and she wishes the straps of the backpack weren't cutting in to her shoulders.

'Mummy, it's cold!' Dawn accuses.

Jean smiles; she's right, there's no denying it. The frozen puddles along the towpath and the clouds of white breath are testament to that. Moisture is freezing into James' hair, and her own fingers are numb.

'Stop whining child' Henry snaps helpfully, and Dawn bursts into tears and howls.

'Come and look at the horsey' Jennifer cajoles.

Dawn stops crying and toddles over to the paddock where the ponies cower beneath their damp shaggy coats. Claire wonders where Jennifer got that equanimity from. Like characters in a Thelwell cartoon, the little round children stand on tiptoe to reach the pony's soft muzzle. It drips mucus onto their outstretched hands as it searches for food in their soggy mittens.

Dawn steps back from the snorts and blusters, and falls through a thin layer of ice. She lands with a startled splosh, and for a few seconds is too surprised to cry. As the cold water seeps through her trousers, she recalls her lung capacity and sets up a loud caterwauling that causes Jean and Claire to come running. The other children cluster around in a circle, unsure what to do, and the men and Joyce are on the fringes of the action, awaiting further commands, hoping they will be sent ahead for provisions.

'Oh, I'll have to take her back to the house, poor thing, she's wet through!' Jean is calm and solicitous.

'I've got a change of clothes in here, you can dry her off and she'll be fine.' Claire whips off the backpack and begins sorting through the carefully organised contents. Dawn draws a short breath and carries on wailing.

'No, really Claire, it'll be for the best. You guys carry on and enjoy your walk. I'll take her home.'

She picks up Dawn who clings to her and buries her head in her shoulder. Safe again, the bawling subsides to sobs. Joyce has already turned to carry on. If small children must fall into puddles, so be it. There is still a cosy pub to walk to and a glass of sherry to be had there. James and Henry murmur acquiesces that this is for the best and if she's sure and okay then. Claire sighs and shoulders the backpack again, looking after Ruth, Adam and Emma, as they scamper ahead, resuming their game which seems to involve trying to hit each other with sticks.

She gives Jean instructions about turning things up and down on the oven, how to turn the hot water on for a bath and which towels to use from the airing cupboard. There is another loud splash and they whirl round to see Jennifer sitting in another puddle. She looks up at them with large, serious eyes.

'I fell in. I'm wet through too.'

Claire and Jean exchange glances and try hard not to laugh.

'Well, it's a good job I've got so many clean and dry things for you.'

'No, no, I think I should go back to the house with Dawn and Aunty Jean and let you carry on with your walk.'

'Really, do you think so?' Claire bends down to her sodden daughter and fishes her out of the icy mud, silently impressed with her determination if slightly surprised by the manipulation.

'Oh yes,' Jennifer nods furiously, 'I think it's for the best.'

Jean is no longer able to contain herself and bursts out laughing. She puts the bemused and hiccoughing Dawn down and takes Jennifer by the other hand.

'Come on then kiddo, let's get you home.'

Jennifer grins.

'Bye bye, mummy,' she waves and skips off with Jean, chattering up at her aunty as she leads the two wet children back across the field.

Claire shakes her head and sighs. She turns to look at the receding backs of the rest of the walking party and hurries to catch up once again.

****

The children are wrapped in blankets, drinking mugs of hot chocolate. Their clothes are spread out in front of the crackling fire. Jean says they can warm them up before they slip into them. They have pulled the curtains against the grey misty day and the room glows cheerily with the Christmas tree in the corner, as smells of roast meats and baking waft through the house.

'I always wanted long hair like yours,' Jean tells Jennifer as she brushes out her hair. Jennifer purrs and stretches under the rhythmic strokes. Claire never has the time to dry her hair this languorously, and wraps it in a turban towel before rubbing it vigorously and yanking a comb through it. There are always another three heads needing attention. Dawn hates having her hair brushed and she lies on the carpet watching through sleepy eyes.

'Hmm, but it was so curly it grew out instead of down. I looked like I had a bush on my head! Your mother caught me trying to iron it straight once.'

Jennifer imagines Aunty Jean with her head on one side on an ironing board.

'Did it work?'

'No,' Jean laughs at the serious enquiry.

'I wouldn't recommend it. I scorched it, and it smelt horrible.'

She wrinkles her nose at the memory and Jennifer copies her. Jean laughs again and kisses her lightly on the tip of her nose. Dawn wriggles closer and receives a kiss too. They curl up contentedly like a mother cat and her kittens.

'Right, hop into your clothes; they should be toasty warm by now.'

The girls squirm into woolly tights and hand-stitched tunics, and take their towels upstairs to put in the washing basket. Jean puts more wood on the fire and dredges up memories of Moonface to keep the children entertained until Claire comes home with plans for dinner and domestic ritual.

Claire sees the brief moment of silence through a chink in the curtains before the three of them are woken by shouts and clamours. Tears spring unbidden to her eyes as James flings open the glass partition doors.

'Gosh it's warm in here. You missed a good walk.'

He brings in the outside world as he rubs his hands briskly. The children tumble into the room, shedding layers of coats and jumpers. Rows of muddy boots are piled up outside to be washed. Claire shrugs off the backpack, which she will sort out later.

'What's for dinner, I'm starving!'

****

The children are wiping up the detritus of dinner and putting things away. Claire takes a large plate and piles up mountains of mince pies. She whips the cream by hand. They are actually all too full to move, but it is Christmas and somehow she thinks there should always be food on the table. There is a basket of fruit and a bowl of nuts. She hates the nuts because bits of shell fly everywhere and she has to clear them up. A box of chocolates also sits on the coffee table; two layers of shiny wrapped treats, which get passed around the room at carefully measured intervals. They don't go far with a houseful and choices must be made carefully. Emma examines the sheet for the longest time; she doesn't want to be stuck with the coffee cream.

Claire finds the cups for the coffee, and loads them onto a tray with the sugar bowl and the milk jug. As soon as the children have dried the spoons, they will be used again. The preparation and clearing away is relentless. Claire wonders if it will ever stop.

They are all wedged into the front room, having been promised another present. Presents are rationed rather than handed out all at once. When the house is full, the ceremony of gift giving can take a week. Claire has got everyone a 'Boxing Day present' and she has distributed all the wrapped rectangles. Books and puzzles seem appropriate for quiet play today.

'Where's yours, Mummy?' Ruth asks her.

'Oh, I haven't got one. It doesn't matter. Go ahead, open it.'

Claire tries not to look at James. She suspects he has forgotten again, as he does every year, but she doesn't want to embarrass him.

'I'm sorry, I didn't think to get you another present.' He looks crestfallen. She really doesn't mind.

'You can share mine, Mummy' Adam offers kindly. She smiles and thanks him, although she'd really rather not. His is a book about how cars work.

After the paper has been tidied away into a box, everyone slumps into position; reading, stencilling, drawing, or working out their puzzles. Henry slips out for a surreptitious pipe although the smoke which clings to him on his return ridicules any notion of secrecy. James wanders off to his study to work on an idea he has for one of his business machines. He thinks he can write something in a new encryption which will make things work faster. Claire sits back and relaxes, closing her eyes against the low murmur of happy children.

She is startled by a short scream.

'Claire, there's a strange man in the house,' Joyce whispers urgently and clutches the arm of the sofa.

'Where, mum?' Claire is perplexed by the thought of this intruder.

'There!' Joyce points frantically as a figure wanders past the door. Although the moulded glass distorts his shape like a sinister fairground mirror, Claire can clearly see the mince pie in his hand.

'Don't be daft, mum, that's only James. He's not that strange!'

Joyce's eyes are wide open and she looks scared.

'Who is he, Claire?'

Suddenly Claire feels a chill. The children are amused, but Claire glances at Jean and they both know it's not funny. She stands and goes to kneel before her mother. She takes Joyce's hands in hers and looks into her frightened eyes.

'That's James, mum, my husband.'

'Husband? But Claire... you haven't got... when did you... why haven't I...'

Claire looks to Jean for help. The children are quiet now. They have stopped laughing and caught something of the atmosphere. Jean speaks slowly.

'You remember, mum. Claire and James got married about ten years ago, it was a beautiful wedding. We all went. That was before the children.'

'Oh yes, the children.' Joyce looks around at the children and smiles, but she doesn't seem to recognise them and they are frightened.

'Come on kids, let's see where Uncle Henry's got to.' Jean ushers them out of the room and they allow themselves to be led meekly into the garden. Claire remains on the floor in front of mother, stroking her hands and willing her to recollect. A tear falls onto her hand as Joyce shakes her head.

'I don't remember, Claire, I don't remember.'

Claire puts her arms around her and gently smoothes her hair. She kisses her head and whispers,

'It's okay mum, it doesn't matter.'

Joyce breaks the embrace and looks up at her daughter.

'Is he good to you?'

Claire smiles, "Yes, mum, he's good to me."

Joyce nods and clasps her hands in her lap.

'That's good then.' She blinks away the tears and sniffs loudly into a handkerchief. She continues to nod as she rearranges her mind. James walks in with a mouthful and stops abruptly.

'Where is everyone? What's all this?'

Claire looks from him to Joyce in alarm. Joyce pats her arm and smiles,

'It's nothing, James. Everything's fine.'

10

Aldwych

Zone 1: Piccadilly (between Holborn & Covent Garden).

Attractions: Charles Dickens' House; Roman Bath; Transport Museum; R Twining and Company Ltd.

Aldwych originally opened in 1907 as Strand station, but underwent a name change in 1917 to allow for a new Strand station on the Northern Line. At various times, works of art from the National Gallery and the British Museum were stored here as a precaution against Zeppelin attacks.

The station was closed in 1940 and one platform served as a public air raid shelter. Service was resumed in 1946, and continued until 1994, when the station was closed due to the perceived uneconomical cost of a lift replacement.

Due to its well-preserved interior and stylish tiling it is a popular location for film and television productions, including The Battle of Britain (1969); Superman IV: The Quest For Peace (1986); The Krays (1990); Patriot Games (1992); The Good Shepherd (2006); and the music video for Firestarter by The Prodigy (1996).

Thomas Twining bought Tom's Coffee House on the Strand in 1706. Coffee houses were places where men gathered to drink, gossip, and conduct business. At the time the most popular drinks in England were coffee, beer and gin. Thomas Twining began selling tea as a point of difference and it gained many fans so that by the 1750s it had become the most popular drink in Britain. Twinings Tea is now an official Royal Warrant holder, supplies tea to the Red Cross for food parcels, and still occupies a shop in the same place.

****

Claire hums to herself. Jennifer looks up and squeezes her hand; she has not seen her mother happy like this for a while. They are going to catch the train, but not for shopping. Usually when they catch the train, they are going to buy luxuries that are beyond their little village like floral print blouses or wallpaper or gardening gloves. Today they are going to an art gallery.

Claire loves art galleries, and she loves catching the train to London. She preferred the steam trains that roared and hissed into the station but these new electric things will do. The train pulls away from the platform and clatters along the tracks. She finds the sound therapeutic and is lulled by its rhythm. Jennifer sits opposite; her legs swinging from the seat and not touching the floor. Claire has to sit forward, so when the train changes direction, they swap seats. It is a ritual that they undertake every time and Jennifer is ready for it, giggling with complicity.

As they leave the countryside behind, the willow-lined river and cow-encrusted fields yield to rows of terraced housing. Jennifer stares out of the window as so much humanity glides by, compressed into narrow streets.

'We used to live in a house like that,' her mother tells her. Jennifer laughs, not quite believing it. She is terrified by the thought that because they all look the same, how would you ever remember which one was yours?

Paddington Station is grand and busy; full of shouts and whistles and the squeal of brakes. When it was opened a hundred years ago, crowds collected to wonder at the architecture of Isambard Kingdom Brunel. Jennifer admires its high and beautiful roof; she doesn't care if it is practical. Claire admires the pomposity of his name. She imagines the dinner ladies calling it out in the playground; 'Stop pushing Isambard Kingdom!' More likely he was a good child and all the others would have to gather round to 'Look at this perfect bridge little Isambard has built from matches and pipe cleaners.'

Under the gleaming span of glass and iron Jennifer is reverential. She shuffles to keep up with her mother, grasping her hand firmly and feeling compelled to whisper. They emerge into the streets and walk through the bustle that is the capital city. Jennifer loves the excitement. They travel on big red double-decker buses and sometimes they get to sit in the front seats. This is a treat and Jennifer pretends to like it, but actually she feels slightly queasy when they pull up in traffic, which they do often. From her angle it seems that the cars below disappear beneath their wheels. She wants to bang on the windows and warn the occupants that they are about to get crushed, but she doesn't like to make a scene and her mother doesn't seem to notice so it must be alright. She sticks instead to enumerating the black cabs, but there are so many that she loses count. When Claire asks her, 'how many now?' she makes up a random number. Claire nods sagely and never points out that it's fewer than last time.

Mornington Crescent

At the Tate Gallery, Claire gazes at the Turners. She loves the expansive canvas; feels the wind and the rain and is dazzled by the sudden outbreaks of sun. She hugs herself to stop from reaching out and touching the globules of oil in ships and sunsets. Fires and storms sweep through the gallery and she finds the destruction thrilling. There are few people to hamper these natural disasters. Shimmering colour renders volcanic eruptions, violent snowstorms and fatal typhoons into something beatific. And then there is the sea. The sea. She can taste the salt spray; she yearns to its call; its limitless horizon and unbounded possibilities.

Jennifer is curled up on a seat, sucking her thumb. She is exhausted by the Pre-Raphaelites with their serene expressions, extravagant scenery and radiant hair. She doesn't understand the deeper themes and mythology but she likes the pretty colours. Claire sits beside her and enjoys the peace. She would like to stay here for a while, in this painted world, but there are things to be done. She wakes Jennifer gently and leads her back through the central dome and porticoed entranceway. It used to be a prison, she thinks; now it is more like a temple. They retrace their steps away from the treasures of London, and gradually their familiar world reasserts itself.

That night Jennifer dreams of flying taxis, steamroller buses and the Lady of Shalott's hair. Claire dreams of drowning.

11

Russell Square

Zone 1: Piccadilly (between King's Cross St Pancras and Holborn).

Nearby Attractions: The Charles Dickens Museum; Coram Fields; The Foundling Museum; Great Ormond Street Hospital; The Horse Hospital.

Great Ormond Street Hospital for Children is a centre of excellence in child healthcare, being the UK's only academic biomedical research centre specialising in paediatrics, and is one of the world's leading hospitals for children. It receives annually over 192,000 patient visits to the hospital.

In 1843, 51,000 people died in London, of whom 21,000 were children under 10. The population had grown following the Industrial Revolution and the end of the wars with Napoleon's France, but the hospital provision had not grown with it and the established hospitals, such as St Bartholomew's and Guys, struggled to cope with the increased demand.

Dr Charles West, an expert on gynaecology and diseases of women and children, founded Great Ormond Street Hospital in 1852. It had ten beds in two wards – one for boys and one for girls – and was the first institution in the UK to offer inpatient care to children only. Many patients probably benefitted from being washed, fed, and kept warm.

Charles Dickens was a friend of Dr West, and he wrote a powerful article in his popular magazine, Household Worlds, to publicise the hospital when it opened. It grew rapidly, and a new purpose-built building was constructed in 1871-75, designed by Edward Barry, son of Sir Charles Barry, the architect of the Houses of Parliament.

As expenses increased, the hospital was funded by subscriptions, donations and funding events such as its Annual Festival Dinner which attracted eminent speakers such as Dickens, Oscar Wilde, senior clergymen and members of the Royal Family. During World War I women doctors were employed for the first time. Traditional aristocratic benefactors were hard-hit by the war and the declining agricultural value of their estates. The financial situation meant the hospital could no longer afford to offer free treatment to children of the poor and a 'pay what you can afford' system was introduced, which continued until 1948.

(Until the NHS was established in 1948, senior medical and surgical staff were not paid; they worked at the hospital alongside their private practices as a social duty and for experience in dealing with large numbers of patients in varied conditions).

In 1929 J.M. Barrie was approached to sit on a committee to help buy some land so the hospital could build a much-needed new wing. He declined to serve on the committee but 'hoped to find another way to help'. Two months later the hospital board learned that Sir James had handed over all his rights to Peter Pan.

In 1897, fifty years after J.M. Barrie died, the copyright on Peter Pan expired, but was subsequently extended to 2007. Lord Callaghan proposed a special amendment to the Copyright, Designs and Patents Act of 1988, which granted the hospital a right to royalties in perpetuity. Barrie requested that the amount raised from Peter Pan would never be revealed, and the hospital has always honoured his wishes, but every time a production of the play is staged, and from the sale of every book and related product, Great Ormond Street receives a royalty.

****

The children are playing Olympics on the green outside, inspired by the heroic feats they have seen in flickering images on the television. Claire watches them out of the window and smiles. Ruth, Adam and Emma have been leaping and sprinting. They fancy the track and field events and imagine themselves as sprinters, hurdlers, high jumpers and long jumpers. The hurdles are kitchen chairs and they look more like they are competing in steeplechase. Claire flinches as they clatter into the furniture and it topples to the ground.

Jennifer walks round and round the square. She is in no hurry and she chatters to her cuddly tiger which accompanies her on her perambulations. Adam tells her that she is being silly by just walking. He says the Olympics are all about being the fastest, jumping the highest or the furthest. Bigger; better; faster; more. Jennifer shrugs.

'We got a gold medal for walking.'

Claire turns away to hide a smile. She's right, they did. They also got a gold medal for swimming and although everyone is terribly proud of Anita Lonsbrough, it's hard to swim without a pool, and no one's parents will let them go down to the river. They have to abandon the yachting, canoeing and sailing too.

Adam limps into the kitchen with a splinter in his foot. Emulating Abebe Bikila, he was loping around the square in bare feet, attempting the world record for the marathon. He decides only Africans can run in bare feet; they must have tough soles. Claire patches him up with TCP and suggests he copy another hero.

'What about Herb Elliot?'

Adam thinks about it for a moment and then leaps up and jogs outside. How quickly he switches allegiance to Australia. Clare shakes her head; her children are fickle. They pretend to box like Cassius Clay and fence like Aladar Gerevich. They are at home with the foreign names and they know the colours of the flags and where they are in the atlas.

They prance and whirl in gymnastic routines. Ruth can cartwheel and pirouette and perform flick-flacks and walkovers. Adam lumbers up onto his hands but falls flat on his back and winds himself. Once again Claire winces, but the children tell her athletes must make sacrifices for their sport. They lay down a skipping rope and pretend it is a beam. Their beam exercise consists of walking up and down in a straight line with an occasional jump or hop. From where Claire is standing, they look as though they are being tested for alcohol consumption, and failing. Emma bounds around doing Arab springs. When she finishes she throws out her arms and sticks out her bottom. Claire wipes the tears of laughter from her eyes.

She doesn't remember the skipping in Rome, but it is one of the most hotly contested events at these Olympics. All the girls from around the square come out with their skipping ropes and their own sets of rules. There is speed skipping and skipping on the spot. This is a performance sport and marks are awarded for technique and interpretation. Claire and Valerie are asked to be the judges and they oblige as they lean against the fence and try to keep a straight face.

'How did you get roped into this?' Claire asks and Valerie swats her on the arm and sniggers. Claire never knew she could be so much fun.

David from up the road wants to play Olympics but only if he can wear his football gear. The children think he is a little bit odd because he likes being in goal. They set up an area for him between two trees and take pot shots at him. He is kitted out in gloves and kneepads and a claret and blue top that comes down to his knees. He dives from side to side saving penalties and free kicks. He thinks he is Colin McDonald, but no one has the heart to tell him that professional footballers can't play in the Olympic Games.

As dusk falls, David heads in for his tea, taking his ball with him. This seems to signal the end of the Games and the children calculate their medals and their new world records as they drift inside. Claire puts down plates of fish cakes in front of them – the breadcrumb encrusted discs look like gold medals to her.

'You are all winners. Well done, I'm proud of you' she tells them, and then,

'Where's Jennifer?'

Ruth sighs,

'She's still walking around the square.'

Claire goes out to fetch her. It is dark now, but Jennifer is happily talking to Tigger.

'It's time to come in, darling.'

'Have I won the walk?'

'Oh yes, you've blitzed the field!'

Jennifer takes her hand and walks inside.

'I'm glad I won, Mummy,' she says seriously, 'But I'm glad it's over.'

She eats her gold medals and salad and ignores her brother. He tells her that no one else joined in her event and so her gold medal doesn't mean anything. Jennifer just smiles an inscrutable smile.

'Just because no one else wanted to do it, doesn't mean it's any less special. And I might not have won one of the others, so I chose wisely, didn't I Mummy?'

'Yes darling, you did.' Claire kisses her upturned nose and shakes her head at her little Olympiads. Where did they get that competitive edge?

12

Tottenham Court Road

Zone 1: Central (between Oxford Circus and Holborn); Northern (between Goodge Street and Leicester Square).

Nearby Attractions: The British Museum; The Cartoon Museum; Seven Dials; Soho.

The British Museum houses objects from all over the world. Founded in 1753, it was established as a museum of human history and culture. The glass-domed Great Court is the largest covered public square in Europe.

The museum's collections include the Elgin Marbles (Parthenon Sculptures), the Rosetta Stone, artefacts from the Sutton Hoo, Egyptian mummies and the Mildenhall Treasure. The location of many of these exhibits is controversial. Among the Greek and Roman sculptures are depictions of headless figures, horses, gods, men, centaurs and battles, and over all hangs the question of should they really be here, free for all to view and admire, or has the museum stolen other peoples' history?

Equally worth preserving are the cartoons, caricatures and comic strips housed in the nearby Cartoon Museum, opened by the Duke of Edinburgh in 2006. While the objects in the British Museum celebrate dignitaries and worthy figures, those in the Cartoon Museum often mock and lampoon the same. Everyone is entitled to their opinion.

If the British Museum displays the static history and culture of humanity, then the adjacent area of Soho reveals its living nature. The established entertainment district, famous for its nightlife, has altered its aspect over the years. Originally settled by many immigrants, it was once known as London's French Quarter when hordes of Huguenots arrived in the late 17th century. By the mid 19th century most of the respectable families had moved away, leaving the area to be populated by prostitutes, music halls, small theatres and cheap eating houses and hostelries.

For much of the 20th century it was mostly renowned for its sex shops, although these were 'cleaned up' in the 1980s as the area once again re-invented itself with fashionable restaurants, media offices and post-production film industries. It has been integral to many stand-up comedy acts and music movements including modern jazz, rock, pop and punk. It also shares its reputation as the capital's gay village with the homes of various ethnic, religious and spiritual groups from the Irish immigrants' Catholic Church to Hare Krishna temples, and London's Chinatown.

Time and fashion appear to dictate morality.

****

James tests the children on their homework. He questions them about the Kings and Queens of England, African countries, French grammar, the Periodic table, the Lakeland poets and the laws of thermodynamics. Claire laughs as she slides another egg onto his breakfast plate. He winks at her; she might know that he can't tell his Wordsworth from his Coleridge but the children have no idea and recite passages about daffodils and Kubla Khan. James nods solemnly and then says,

'Oh I don't know; it's all Keats to me!' laughing at his own joke as the children roll their eyes and Claire groans in mock pain.

He is more serious about scientific matters and drills them over atoms, vectors and wave motion.

'So, if hot air rises, why is it cold up the top of mountains?'

They all look at Jennifer who has neatly pushed the food into separate piles on her plate. Having first attacked the mushrooms, she is now attending to the bacon. The fried bread is her favourite and she saves it until last, if she can protect it from Adam's predatory fork.

'That's a very interesting question, Jennifer.' James' eyes gleam as he gazes around the table.

'Well, who can tell her?'

Ruth looks out of the window. Sometimes they get woodpeckers in the garden and they all dash to the window to look. She wishes one would arrive now.

Emma suggests,

'Is it something to do with pressure?'

James nods and encourages her to go on, but she falters. Adam picks up the challenge.

'Hot air is less dense than cold air? And gravity forces cold air down so that hot air can take its place?'

'Yes, but why is hot air less dense?' James probes. He begins moving the salt cellar and the butter dish around on the table, feeling an example coming on.

'Because God made it that way.' There is no question in Jennifer's voice. She is simply stating something she has been taught at school.

'Don't be ridiculous; there's no such thing as God.'

There is a solid thunk as Claire puts down the skillet.

'James, a word, now.'

She goes into the hallway and stands with her hands balled into fists on her hips. James finishes his mouthful, wipes his mouth and smiles at the children.

'Close the door, please,' she says quietly, and he shrugs and shuts the children into the kitchen. They look at each other in wide-eyed silence and they can hear through the thin wall.

'What's all this about, Claire?' he laughs.

'Don't tell her that there is no such thing as God.'

'Well, there's not.' Suddenly James becomes serious too. 'I don't know why we send her to that school anyway, filling her head with religious claptrap.'

'She can have her own opinions, can't she?'

'Not when she's wrong!'

Claire snorts and folds her arms, 'Oh, I see, now we come down to it. That is so arrogant! Just because someone disagrees with you, they're wrong, is that it?'

'Calm down Claire, for Christ's sake!'

'I will not calm down. This is important. You can't just make them all into little yous.'

'That's not what I'm trying to do.'

'Isn't it?' Claire glares at him.

'No, but I will not have any child of mine believing in that crap!'

'In case you've forgotten, she's my child too, and she can believe what she wants to believe.'

'But Claire, there's no scientific proof; it's all just a load of rubbish.' James holds out his palms in a supplicating gesture.

'For God's sake, James, sometimes there's more to life than scientific proof. You don't have to like it, but you do have to live with it.'

When they come back into the kitchen, James isn't smiling anymore. Jennifer pushes the fried bread around her plate. Adam looks from one to the other, while Emma stares at the floor. Ruth bursts into giggles and Adam kicks her under the table. Claire thinks there's a reason people say you should never talk about sport, politics or religion at the dinner table. This was only breakfast. Hot air keeps on rising.

****

Claire straightens the pans. There is no reason why she has to keep watch; everything is primped and primed and will be ready at the right time. The children have gathered in the kitchen. It is the warmest place in the house; she has shut the hatch doors and turned up all the gas rings. James complains about wasted heating, but James isn't home from work yet.

Ruth and Adam have exams coming up and are meant to be studying. Adam has art and he is sketching designs on a big pad. They are doodles and concepts that he can explain so that the lines take on meaning and are more than just charcoal marks on a white page. Ruth is chewing a pencil. A physics book sits on the table in front of her and she frowns as she neatly underlines passages. Emma colours in a geology map of the British Isles.

The bold clashing colours remind Claire of curtains and she sighs as she thinks they must reupholster the sofa. She would like a new one, but she knows that James will say they can't afford it. She likes new things; she is sick of making do and mending; it seems to her to be the story of her life. She remembers the maps she learned at school, with vast swathes of the world still covered in pink – The British Empire before it was carved up.

Jennifer fills in the jam tarts. Claire makes the pastry and allows her to roll it out. Jennifer crowds as many round shapes as she can fit into the pale disc, creating a circular mound and gathering the scraps, squishing them together and stretching them out again into a new shape, as though all the leftovers can be remoulded into something useful. Just like The British Empire, Claire thinks ruefully. When Jennifer has pressed the pastry circles into their cases, she fills them individually. She travels the teaspoons of homemade jam up one side, across, down, and back in ever decreasing rectangles. She never does one out of order and they all get exactly the same careful measure – no random dollops.

'Dum de dum de dum de dum…' The children look at each other and smile. They must be quiet now as their mother listens to *The Archers* as she does every day at this hour. They have learned not to ask questions or have needs during the minutes Claire slips away to Ambridge. She listens with her head tilted to one side to the incidents at Brookfield Farm. She stirs the gravy to rioting saboteurs, kidnappings, fires, robberies, plane crashes, and fights outside The Bull. It's all happening in the otherwise sleepy Midland village. When it finishes she shakes her head as if emerging from her daily dream and tells the children to wash their hands and face and lay the table. She pops the tray of tarts and an apple pie into the oven and checks the kitchen clock. They will be ready in time for dessert, and she shoos the children to dinner.

****

'Okay, you may begin,' James announces from the head of the table. Claire mutters grace to herself. She knows there is no way James will countenance it being said aloud. She says it as she carries the last things to the table; the bread rolls and the gravy boat. She nods at James as she sits and spreads the napkin across her lap. It is really her who starts the meal, but she doesn't want the children to think their father is being undermined.

It's been a difficult day. In the morning they went to visit James' parents. Ruth is going though her 'difficult phase' and none of the children really want to spend time with the grandparents anyway. At a rather fraught lunch of quiche and salad the topic of piercing had come up again. Claire has made it very clear that Ruth cannot get her ears pierced until she is eighteen. She made this rule some time ago, hoping that Ruth would forget. She hasn't. As she persisted to plead her case, Claire finally snapped,

'Only tarts get their ears pierced.'

Ruth smirked and asked with false innocence,

'Is Grandma a tart, then?'

Adam had spluttered lettuce all over the table and even James looked as though he might laugh. Claire had glanced at the garnet studs in James' mother's earlobes and back pedalled furiously. It was a good point, she had to admit, but not in public. They would have sent Ruth to her room, but they couldn't if they weren't in their own house so they left under what she thought to be a cloud, although James had seemed quite happy at the prospect and Ruth folded her arms smugly in the back seat, the others looking at her with a new respect.

With extra time on his hands, James has been 'doing correspondence'. This means he has been seated at the table surrounded by piles of paper and cups of tea. Once he discovered that he had paid fractionally more tax than he should have, so now he does his own accounts. Shoeboxes full of papers and receipts become covered in spidery handwriting and scraps blossom with columns of figures. He becomes all flailing elbows, wild hair and bad temper as he wrestles with fringe benefits, sundries and miscellaneous. The children take it in turns to tiptoe forward with a fresh brew at regular intervals. He acknowledges them with a brief nod and they scarper back to the relative safety of the kitchen. It's a tense time for everyone.

'Did you get all your correspondence done?' Claire asks.

She knows he has, because he is smiling and genial, so she knows she can broach the subject.

'I certainly did' he says, helping himself to slices of roast beef. 'What has everyone else been up to this afternoon?' He looks around the table and his eyes alight on Ruth.

'Revising' she shrugs.

'Revising what?'

'Physics.'

'Aha,' he says, leaning forward with interest. 'What in particular?'

'The movement of heat energy,' Ruth wavers. She knows she is about to be tested, and she wishes she had made something else up.

'Well, you know that heat energy moves in three ways.'

Ruth nods, dumbly, miserably. She knows he will ask her what they are.

'What are they?'

'Conduction, convection and radiation.'

'Excellent,' James approves. 'And what is the difference?'

'Well, conduction is when energy is passed directly from one item to another; convection is… convection is…'

James waits. Nothing is forthcoming.

'Could you pass the carrots, please, darling?' Claire asks Emma, who picks up the orange dish and hands it to her. She smiles, 'Thank you.'

James frowns briefly and then claps his hands. The children glance at each other. He has got an idea.

'I've got an idea. Let's play 'conduction, convection, and radiation'. When you want someone to pass you something, you have to ask for it by conduction, convection or radiation. If it's conduction, everyone has to pass it from hand to hand around the table, indicating the passage of heat directly from one item to another, as you said. For convection, someone has to get up, walk around the table and deliver it to you, and if it's radiation, they can throw it at you.'

'James,' Claire cautions, 'I've gone to a lot of trouble with the dinner.'

'It's okay,' he laughs. 'It's a way to make them learn.' He turns to Adam, 'Could you radiate me a Yorkshire pudding please?'

Adam hesitates briefly, then picks one up and lobs it gently across the table. James catches it neatly and cheers.

'Hurrah! Who else needs some food?'

'I'd like some carrots by convection, please,' says Emma.

James picks them up and walks around the table to place them in front of her. He grins as peas and carrots are passed from hand to hand, butter and pepper are walked around the table and bread rolls and roast potatoes fly through the air.

Jennifer pipes up, 'May I have some gravy, please?'

'How do you want it?' James asks with a smile.

'I don't know; I'm not doing physics.'

'Come on, we're all playing,' he says.

Jennifer shrugs, 'What are the options?'

'Conduction, convection and radiation,' the children and James chorus together.

Jennifer bites her lip anxiously, 'Um...radiation?'

The gravy boat sails across the table and she ducks. It crashes against the framed portrait of The Queen and the thick brown liquid slides down her gown and the wall.

'Oh, James!' Claire is exasperated. Jennifer bursts into tears. Emma and Adam are shocked. Ruth giggles.

'She was meant to catch it!' James sounds bemused.

'I'm sorry,' Jennifer wails as Claire goes to get a dustpan and brush and collect the shards of pottery and rich brown perfectly unlumpy gravy.

'It's not your fault, sweetheart,' Claire assures her. 'There's more gravy.'

'But I broke the gravy boat,' she sobs.

'No you didn't, that was your father with his stupid games.'

At the head of the table, James looks crestfallen.

'But, they've got to learn.'

13

Kings' Cross St Pancras

Zone 1: Circle (between Euston Square and Farringdon, towards Edgware Road); Hammersmith and City (between Euston Square and Farringdon, towards Barking); Metropolitan (between Euston Square and Farringdon, towards Aldgate); Northern (between Euston and Angel); Piccadilly (between Russell Square and Caledonian Road); Victoria (between Euston and Highbury and Islington). Connections with National Rail.

Nearby attractions: The British Library; London Canal Museum.

Even without the fictional Platform Nine and Three-Quarters destination Hogwarts, King's Cross St Pancras is London's third busiest station, serving more lines than any other. It's also had more than its fair share of recent tragedies; a fire in 1987 killed thirty-one people when a lit match fell into an escalator machine room, and in July 2005, a bomb attack on a Piccadilly line train travelling between King's Cross St Pancras and Russell Square left twenty-six people dead.

St Pancras was born Pancratius at Phrygia in AD 290. When he was 14 the orphaned boy was taken to Rome by his uncle where he converted to Christianity. Shortly afterwards, during the Diocletian persecution of the Christians) he was beheaded in Via Aurelia for publicly declaring his faith. Pope Vitalian sent relics across to England, hoping they would help act as objects of worship in the new churches being built – St Pancras Old Church is one of the oldest sites of Christian worship in England. St Pancras is the patron saint of children and the champion of oaths and treaties. He is invoked against false witness, perjury, cramps and headaches.

The nearby London Canal Museum offers an insight into another form of transport about the city, as well as featuring the history of the ice trade and ice cream. Also in the area is the post-modern red brick building of the British Library, which houses over twelve million books and manuscripts including the Magna Carta, an illustrated Canterbury Tales and a First Folio of Shakespeare's works. The Library possesses a collection of the rarest classical stamps in the world, as well as precious manuscripts, drafts, artwork, letters and song lyrics. From JK Rowling to John Lennon; Charles Dickens to Carol Anne Duffy; Enid Blyton to George Bernard Shaw; and Thomas Hardy to Posy Simmonds, the repository is a haven of inspiration.

****

Claire breathes deeply. She loves the smell of polished wood and cool stone. Motes of dust drift in coloured shafts of light and it is as though she can see the air itself. Of course she can't; James would scoff at the notion. There is history in the dust; thousands of years of it. This could make her feel insignificant, as though her problems don't matter, but it doesn't. She feels a part of it. She feels as though she belongs.

James has the children. He has taken them to learn to canoe on the river, or to play football on the fields, or to climb trees in the woods. She doesn't even know where they are, but she knows they are safe and so she doesn't care. There are things she should be doing at home. The washing basket is overflowing as always and there is tonight's dinner to prepare and the housework to be done. There will be more clouds of dust in her home than here. She was going to make jam from the plums and bake a batch of biscuits to last them the week. She needs to do the ironing and sew the buttons back on James' shirts – she doesn't know how he manages to pull them off the cuffs. So many things she should be doing.

But Claire doesn't move. She lets her head rest on the pew in front of her and her head fills with stillness. She loves the silence of this calm, quiet church most of all. She can be alone with her thoughts, even if she can't remember what they are. She doesn't pray – there is nothing in particular that she wants. She just allows the peace and joy to seep into her soul through osmosis. She never comes to the services. They are at inappropriate times and she can't bring the children. They would fidget and complain and James wouldn't like it. He thinks they should be outside, being active.

She looks up at the altar, lit by the stained-glass window. She likes how plain the place is, without any bleeding icons cruelly nailed to crucifixes to remind us of our sins. She knows what they are; she doesn't need to be constantly told how miserable she is; she understands the nature of sacrifice. This is somehow uplifting and reassuring. The flowers are fresh and colourful, suggesting hope and promise. She doesn't know all the correct responses, but she feels accepted as she sits in silence.

She thumbs through a hymnbook, inhaling the scent of solace. The pages are edged with gilt and she lets them slip between her fingers, fanning her face. Random words catch her eye; valiant; hopefulness; rejoice; forgive; peace; everlasting love. She sings the hymns quietly and makes up tunes to fit the ones she doesn't know. She closes her eyes. She wants to stay cocooned inside this world of comforting ritual. She doesn't believe in confession; but she leaves with a new spring in her step and a smile on her face.

****

'We've something to tell you.' Jean looks shy as she sits across the table from them, her fingers interlaced with Henry's.

'Oh yes?' Claire takes a sip of tea and tucks her feet beneath her. The children are in bed, the dinner things are cleared away, tomorrow's lunches have been made, and she can relax.

'We're going to go and live in America.'

'Well! When?' James is ever practical. He may be surprised but he immediately counters with logistics.

'In a couple of weeks. Hal has got a job with a construction company.'

'Congratulations!' James shakes Henry's hand.

'Thank you,' he smiles. 'You've been great. We appreciate all your help and letting us stay and everything. But now it's time to move on, and the opportunity came up, and I couldn't let it go. Of course, you can come and visit any time.'

'Great. That's great!' James is genuinely beaming. Claire nods. She knows there is no way they will take four children across the ocean.

'Where is the job?' James asks.

'California.' Jean is looking at Claire, searching for a response. 'I've never been and it will be so exciting.'

'It's a big project, working on accommodation for the university at Berkeley. They're expanding with all the students there and everything. They've asked me to be foreman. Some of the guys from New York are involved and they remembered me from before.'

'That's fantastic news. Well done. I hear they're doing amazing research there.'

Henry shrugs. He will not be involved with the research. He is not interested in the minds so much as the bodies that house them.

'Claire, you haven't said anything. Are you happy for us?' Jean takes her hand.

'Of course I'm happy for you. It's a fantastic opportunity.' Claire pats her hand absently and then pushes herself up from the table. 'I'll put the kettle on.'

'Sod the kettle! This calls for a celebration. Why don't we go down the pub?' James grins and claps his hands together. Claire smiles at his evident excitement at the thought of physicists playing with neutrons and alpha particles and bouncing atoms off the wall in their laboratories, or whatever it is they do.

Henry and James grab their coats; it seems like as good a reason as any. Henry is halfway out of the door before he turns back to Jean.

'Aren't you coming?'

'No, I should stay here, with Claire.'

Mornington Crescent

'Don't be silly!' Claire shoos her out of the door. 'Go and celebrate, I'll be fine!'

'If you're sure?' Jean wavers.

'Of course I'm sure. Go on, they won't wait!' She's right. James and Henry have already set off down the lane. Their voices recede into the dark.

Jean hugs Claire briefly and fiercely, before kissing her on the cheek.

'Thanks, sis,' she whispers.

Claire nods, 'Go!'

Jean wrestles her arms into her coat and races out the front door. It slams behind her and Claire stands in the kitchen, alone.

****

Claire hears them come in although she pretends to be asleep. James stumbles into bed and throws his arm around her, pulling her warm body towards him. His breath smells of beer, but Claire quite likes it. He kisses her shoulder.

'I missed you tonight.'

'Hmm.'

'I'm happy for them. And for us too. We'll have our house back. I mean, I don't mind that they've been here, but now we can get on with our family. Emma can move into that room and she won't have to share with Jennifer anymore. She'll love that!'

'Hmm.'

He runs his hand down her side, smoothing his palm over the dip and curve of her soft hip and thigh.

'It'll be just us again.'

Claire shifts slightly, and James knows that she is awake. He turns her to face him and props himself on his elbow. He strokes her hair from her face, covering her cheeks, nose and mouth with soft beery kisses.

'She'll be okay. She's a big girl now. Just because you're the big sister, you don't have to look after her all your life. She'll be fine. I know things didn't work out before when she left, but they're good now. Hal seems to be responsible. He'll take care of her. And Dawn.'

He kisses her more urgently, cupping her breast in his hand. His fingers caress her nipple and he circles his hand down over her belly and slides it between her legs. His breath is warm and moist as he whispers into her ear.

'You don't have to worry about her. She'll be fine. Honestly.'

Claire throws her arms around him and buries her face in his neck. 'But what about me?' she thinks.

PART THREE

21st October '60

Dear Jean,

It feels strange to be writing to you again after all this time. Remember the letters I used to write you from London? We had no furniture and I had to sit on an upturned milk crate and balance the letter on my knee! Well, now at least we have a table so I am ensconced in the cosy kitchen.

I am glad you arrived safely and I hope you are well. I miss you being around the house, and I know that Jennifer misses Dawn because she trails around the place like a lost puppy. The children are outside looking for hedgehogs, although any self-respecting hedgehog would be tucked up somewhere they can't get at it. We had one snuffling around in the garden the other night and I put out a saucer of milk for it. I don't know if that's what you're meant to feed them, but it had all gone in the morning so I suppose something must have drunk it.

I have some sad news, I'm afraid. Manderlay died a couple of days ago. Of course, she was a very old cat and she died peacefully in her sleep, so it could have been worse. I always swore I would never get another cat after Grimalkin, because you get so attached to them and it is so sad when they die, but this one was James' really.

We wrapped her in her favourite blanket and buried her in the garden. James dug a big hole, although not the six foot that Adam kept insisting it should be, and we all stood around and cried. I thought it might be a nice idea to plant some flowers on the grave, so we planted out an 'M' shape in daffodil bulbs, although they probably won't all come up and I'll have to sneak out with a potted plant when no one's looking and pretend. Adam said that dead bodies made great compost and the flowers would spring up in no time. I think he was trying to be helpful but it set Jennifer off all over again and she wouldn't stop bawling.

Then in the night she came in to our bedroom because she had a nightmare that worms were wriggling all over Manderlay, which really isn't all that nice. I tried to assure her that we had wrapped her tightly in her blanket so nothing would get in there. James muttered that she was dead anyway so wouldn't feel a thing, which I'm not sure was all that helpful. Jennifer asked if she'd gone to heaven and James just grunted – you know how he feels about these things. I had to take her back to bed and tuck her in and promise her that Manderlay was playing happily with all the other cats in heaven and merrily chasing mice. She seemed satisfied with that and drifted back off to sleep, although I don't think this can be very nice for the mice, but I didn't want to say so. She doesn't seem to care about the mice.

I suppose I had better go and get dinner ready. We're having chops and baked potatoes with bean stew. I don't mind cooking, but it's planning the meals that I hate. I have to think about it every day and make sure we've got enough to last the week and that the children are getting a good mixture of meat and vegetables, and James loves

Mornington Crescent

his puddings. I feel like I'm always in the shop or the kitchen. Anyway, that's enough from me, I sound like a boring old housewife.
 Please write soon.
 Lots of love as always,

Claire

12th December '60

Dear Jean,

I hope you are well and settling in nicely. Please write and tell me how everything is. What is the weather like over there? Are you anywhere near the sea? How is Henry's job? What do you do with yourself and how does Dawn like it? Does she go to school there?

Last weekend we took the children up to London for a pre-Christmas treat. It was madness. So many people were bustling and jostling carrying big bags of shopping. I was too scared to go into any shops in case I lost any of the children. I'd forgotten what a big place it is and there are so many people always in a hurry. Besides, James can't abide shopping so he wouldn't have allowed me to browse. I scarcely got to glimpse what was in the shop windows. It's probably just as well. Everyone seems to be wearing glamorous clothes and short skirts, and I can't do that anymore. Four children have certainly made their mark on my figure, so it looks like it's long dresses and capes for me!

We went to Madame Tussaud's and the Planetarium, which certainly kept us busy all day. James loved the Planetarium, even more than the children I think. He sat there with his head thrown back gazing at the constellations and on the way home he kept trying to point them out and test the children if they could remember what they were. Of course, they couldn't. Ruth could remember the ones that are used for the zodiac signs and she kept saying things were Cancer and Gemini and James got cross. I just thought they were wonderful. The roof seemed to revolve so that you felt as though you were spinning through time and the night was all around you. I'm sending a packet of stars which are supposed to glow in the dark. There's an astronomical chart so you can put them up on the ceiling in their proper configuration if you want, or you can just scatter them at random. I thought Dawn might like them.

There was a long queue at Madame Tussaud's, where we went first to see the waxworks. In the entrance there's a desk with a couple of waxwork dummies behind it, looking for all the world like real people having a bit of a natter. The children started to fidget so James told Emma to go and ask them if the ticket was valid for both places while we waited in the queue. She went up to the desk and said 'excuse me' several times, getting louder each time as she got no response. Other people in the queue started looking at her and laughing and she got very embarrassed when she realised. I'm sure she's not the first child to do it. It was a pretty mean trick on James' behalf, and she sulked for the rest of the day.

I thought the statues were fantastic. There is a beautiful tableau of the royal family. The Queen and Prince Philip are surrounded by their children. Jennifer said, 'There are four of them, mummy, just like us.' Not quite, darling! All the costumes are so good and the waxworks look really lifelike. There's a chamber of horrors too with all sorts of gruesome and grisly things in it, like murderers and serial killers, but of course the children wanted to go. I held Jennifer's hand, but she was terrified and very quiet all the way round. She turned white when she saw the guillotine and the Jack the Ripper exhibit, and I had to rush her out of there before she fainted. The others loved it, and when they came out with James, they filled her in on all the terrible details she might have managed to miss.

In the evening, after dinner, I caught her letting all the water out of the bath that I had run for her. I was cross at first because it takes quite a while for the immersion to heat up, but she was in tears and looked really scared, so I asked her what was the matter and it all came out. In the Chamber of Horrors there's an exhibit about John Haigh, you know, the acid bath murderer. She had somehow got it into her head that we were poisoning her at dinner and then trying to dissolve her in the bath! I didn't know whether to laugh or cry. Where does she get these ideas from? Of course, I let her fill her own bath and promised her we would never hurt her, but I thought no wonder she has such bad dreams and sleepwalks, if that's the sort of thing she thinks about, poor little love.

We're going to bring mum down to stay with us over Christmas, so hopefully that will be alright. She seems a bit better these days, but I'm not sure whether that is because she really is better or because she's learned how to cover up. She loves to see the grandchildren, though, so I'm sure it will do her good. We will miss you all and hope you have a really happy time together.

All my love as always,

Claire

15th December '60

Dear Claire,

This is just a quick note to say Merry Christmas! I hope you all have a great time. Things are pretty hectic here. Hal is working hard and is away all hours on site. We are having a Christmas dinner here for all the guys who work on construction, so I'm going to be busy – I always get the timing wrong and the vegetables are ready way before the meat and some things are cold while others are burned. Hal used to claim that he loved my cooking, but that was when we were courting and now he doesn't have to be so polite. I am only used to cooking for us so have no idea how I'm going to manage for such a large group. How you manage every night with your family plus when you have guests, I'll never know.

We had Thanksgiving at one of Hal's colleague's places. That's bigger than Christmas out here. They have turkey and all the trimmings. All of the vegetables are called different names here. Aubergine is called eggplant (Why? It's got nothing to do with eggs). Courgettes are called zucchinis and some pumpkins are called squash. What we call squash, they call cordial, and they drink pop or soda which is fizzy drink. They also drink this stuff called Kool-Aid which is brightly coloured and full of sugar, and all the kids love it.

At Thanksgiving they eat sweet potatoes, which taste weird and pumpkin pie which tastes delicious but just sounds weird! Everyone sits around saying what they're thankful for. It felt strange because you're meant to spend it with family, so of course I thought of you, even though you're so far away now. All the men then sat around with beers watching baseball on television. They have such massive televisions here now, you wouldn't believe it! And the fridges are huge with separate freezers. Everyone just seems to have so much stuff, I suppose it's cheap or something and they all go round to each others' houses rather than out to the pub or the pictures.

They watch a lot of baseball which takes all day! I can understand wanting to watch football or something which only takes a couple of hours, but this goes on forever. Hal has made a lot of friends on the job – he can talk to anyone, so it seems as though we are always being invited places, and then everyone wants me to say things so that they can listen to my accent which they say makes them laugh. The women don't really watch the game but they all sit out in the garden or the kitchen, and the children run around screeching and creating havoc. Lots of houses have a separate room for their giant televisions – they call it the den or the family room. It's a far cry from James in his study where everything is quiet and still.

It's strange to think of it being Christmas because it is still so warm here. It never really gets cold, so there will be no falling through puddles this year. There is so much fruit and it's all so big. I think everything in California is big. And it's sunny and warm, like a sort of paradise.

Dawn has certainly taken to it. She goes to school here and comes back with all sorts of different words and phrases. She is a proper little mimic. I'm really trying hard to fit in and speak their language. I don't want to be different and I want to know how things are done here so I can do them too and Hal will be proud of me.

We had to buy all the stuff Dawn needed for school – we were given a list and we had to check what all the things were. It was like a little treasure hunt, did you know they call rubbers erasers over here? Rubbers are something else, and not what you would want your daughter to take to school in her pencil case! Really, sometimes you 'realize' that this really is a foreign country.

Love to all,

Jean

19ᵗʰ January '61

Dear Jean,

Thank you very much for the Christmas card and for the money that you sent to the children. We took it down to the building society and exchanged it for pounds which we put into their accounts. Emma in particular loves to see the columns in her passbook which show how much money she has in there. It's not a lot, but it has gained a tiny amount of interest since she last went in, and she was so excited! I am enclosing all their thank you letters that they wrote, so hopefully you'll get a nice big parcel to remind you of us all back here.

Well, here we are, at the beginning of another new year. They seem to fly by now and the children are growing like weeds! They are always growing out of their clothes and I seem to be constantly letting down hems, darning jumpers and sewing on buttons. We got them all some new clothes for Christmas but goodness knows how long they will last. I knitted them all some new hats and scarves too. I have to make the most of it as I know that soon they won't want to wear anything I've made but will be clamouring for shop bought. Ruth has already started to look down her nose at things I wear and she spends her pocket money on patterns and material. She is an excellent sewer and can run up things that look really flash but cost hardly anything. She has a paper round and saves up her money to spend on looking nice – I worry that she might be a handful.

We had a pleasant time at Christmas. James enjoyed the break from work and he set little puzzles for the children. He makes them work out clues, which are usually mathematical equations which relate to letters which in turn are anagrams of places where their presents are hidden. It takes them all day, which keeps them occupied and out of mischief. Jennifer wrote to Father Christmas asking him what reindeers really eat when they're not being fed mince pies and sherry, and James looked it all up in the encyclopaedia and wrote a reply. The only problem now is that Jennifer thinks Father Christmas and James have very similar handwriting and she is not sure whether they are brothers or whether Father Christmas doesn't exist. I overheard Ruth telling her not to let us know that she was having doubts, or no one would get any more presents from Father Christmas! So, we just all go on pretending.

Mum was hard work. She kept forgetting where she was and getting confused. I asked her to make us all a pot of tea and she just kept boiling the kettle over and over again. Each time it boiled, she just looked at it curiously as though she didn't recognise it. She enjoyed the Boxing Day walk though and her feet carried her directly to the pub without any problem, so it can't be too bad. We didn't stay long though, because it was raining and the children were outside in the beer garden with lemonade and packets of crisps. Most of the time, mum read her mystery novels. The one good thing is, she can't remember whodunit, so she can read them again and be none the wiser! I know this sounds flippant and I really don't mean it, but if I think too much about her losing her memory and forgetting things I will get so sad, that this is the only way I can cope.

We did have a little bit of excitement last week. I had dropped Adam and Jennifer at the library and was going to run some errands in town. Adam also wanted to look in the sports shop so I told him I would meet him at the post office and then we could come and collect Jennifer on our way back. Anyway, I found Adam with Jennifer outside the post office looking frantic. Apparently he had told Jennifer not to tell me, but that girl can't keep a secret and it all came tumbling out. She had wandered away from the library having a vague idea that she was meant to meet us, but she didn't know where. A policeman had found her wandering up the high street crying and so he popped her in the back of the car and cruised up and down with her until she spotted Adam and he let her go!

I didn't know what to say because I was cross with Jennifer. It's naughty to wander off like that and she could have got into trouble, but she seemed so sorry and upset about her adventure. I sent her upstairs and told her that her father would have something to say about it when he got home. I never threaten the children with punishment from their father because I want them to see him as a fun person and not ever to be scared of him, but I needed some time to think about it. Anyway, I needn't have worried because when I told James he burst out laughing. Jennifer had cried all afternoon and given herself hiccoughs so we agreed to say no more about it. I had to phone the police station and apologise for wasting their time, although they didn't seem to mind a bit. I hope it's the only time any child of mine will need to be picked up by the police!

That's it from us. We hope you are all well.

All my love as always,

Claire

4th March '61

Dear Jean,

How are you? I hope you are well and that you had a good Christmas and New Year. We were thinking of you being all warm and sunny as we shivered through winter, although it has started to warm up a bit now. I do love England in spring with the daffodils and the lambs gambolling in the fields. Of course it always seems to snow just after they are all born and you hear of them perishing in the cold. Jennifer loves watching them play and Adam teases her if we have lamb (which is not very often because it is so expensive) that she is eating the 'poor little lambies' and then there are tears. Last week she informed me, rather primly I thought, that she wanted to be a vegetarian because animals were her friends and she didn't eat her friends. I'm afraid I was in a bit of a bad mood and I snapped that she would have to make her own meals in that case. It seems to have done the trick anyway, because I've not heard any more about it.

I am having driving lessons, so that I can go up and visit mum. I write to her every week (just a short note with what the children have been up to, so she can keep in mind who we all are) but think I should try to see her more often. And you'll never guess who's teaching me. Valerie! I know that's quite a turn up for the books, but I've seen quite a bit of her and she's a lot nicer than we used to think. Her two girls are a bit older than Adam and Ruth, so it's nice to have someone to talk to about bringing them up and the problems they have. I often worry that I'm not very good at being a mum but when we have tea together she relates the woes she's had with hers (I won't go into it but there was a pregnancy scare recently!) and I think that mine aren't so bad after all.

Anyway, she picks me up in her little Ford Anglia on Wednesday afternoons and teaches me how to drive. It's quite exciting, but I'm also scared being in charge of this big machine that could kill people! She says I mustn't think of it like that, because lots of people drive every day and there are very few accidents, but I still feel a bit nervous. I must admit that when there is a tight gap I sometimes shut my eyes to see if I can squeeze through. It gets my heart racing, although when I picked Jennifer up from school, she curled up on the back seat and went to sleep. I suppose I should take strength from this, because it must mean that she trusts me and I am a safe driver.

Adam and Emma are both doing really well at school and are top of their classes. Adam plays football and Emma plays hockey so they are constantly busy with sport and homework. Ruth doesn't seem to enjoy hers so much though, and I have a parents' evening next week which I'm not really looking forward to. She passes her tests, just, but she just isn't interested. We'll see. I hope Dawn is enjoying her school and making lots of friends.

Jennifer is always talking about this person or that person as though her little friends are the most important thing in her life. I suppose they are.

Please write and let us know how you are getting on.

Love as always,

Claire

12th April '61

Dear Jean,

Hello there. I hope you are well and that everything is okay, we haven't heard from you for a while, but you are always in my thoughts.

I went to a parents' evening for Ruth a couple of weeks ago, and it seems she has been skipping a few lessons here and there and getting behind with her work. It was the first I had heard of it and I thought there must be some mistake, as I would know wouldn't I? Well, apparently not. I questioned her about it when I got home and she began by denying everything, but then it all came out.

She is being bullied at school by some of the girls in her class. They do terrible things like pass a piece of paper around with "I hate Ruth" written on it and everyone signs it and they leave it on her desk at the end of the lesson. Or they write things about her on the blackboard so that she sees them when she comes into class. They trip her up in the corridors, or they won't talk to her at lunchtime and they turn their backs on her when she comes near.

Her favourite thing at school is needlework and she's really very good at it, but last week, they went through her bag and ripped apart the latest blouse she was working on and emptied a pot of ink all over her schoolbag so that she can't put anything in it without it coming out all stained. At games they never pick her to be in their team even though she is very good at sport and one of the fastest runners at the school.

I was furious and nearly cried when she told me. She says there is no reason why they pick on her, and she doesn't know what to do, so she has missed a few days at school to avoid them. I can hardly blame her for that. I feel like such a terrible mother. How could I not have known? And why would anyone want to bully her? She's such a kind and lovely child. I suppose that might make her an easy target. I tried to tell her to ignore them, but her friends have always been so important to her, that she's really upset when they say they don't like her or won't let her play. She's busy at the weekends with her paper round and she baby-sits for the people over the road and does all sorts of odd jobs, so sometimes she seems so grown up.

Now she's talking about leaving school as soon as possible and getting a job in a shop. I want her to stay and pass her exams and go to college, but she put her foot down and said no. She looked so stubborn and determined that she reminded me of you. I almost feel as if I am being punished for refusing to go out to work when I was younger and giving mum all that trouble when I went down to London to study. James says that it's her life and she has to make her own decisions, but she's still so young. She's only a child and I worry about her.

Speaking of mum, I went up to visit last weekend, and things were not good. I have passed my driving test, which is one bright spot as it means I can drive myself up there while James stays at home with the children. I think she has been trying to entice a hedgehog or something, as there are bowls of rotten bread and sour milk all over the place, and some sort of animal droppings which I daren't examine too closely.

I had to clean the house from top to bottom and clear out all the mouldy food in her fridge. I'm not sure that she's eating properly, although she insists that she is. She certainly hasn't washed her sheets or her clothes for a while, and I wonder if she remembers to take a bath. I ran one for her when I was there and when she got into it, I whipped her clothes away and washed them and laid her out new ones to wear. We went shopping for some new tights and underwear, but she got quite cross with me and told me I was treating her like a child.

I filled her cupboards with tins as I don't know how long the fresh produce will keep, but this was the worst visit yet. I felt guilty leaving her, but James says we can't have her to stay with us as the house is too full as it is and the children are too boisterous for her to cope with. I just feel as though I am letting everyone down. I'm sorry this is such a depressing letter, but I've just had a really bad few weeks.

I hope things are better for you and that you are enjoying life in California.

With love as always,

Claire

18th June '61

Dear Jean,

Well, things have been pretty rough here and I really needed to hear from you, but you are obviously too busy to write.

Last time I wrote I think I told you things weren't going very well with mum. Well, they've got worse. I had a call from the police who had found her wandering the streets in her housecoat late at night. It turns out that she had gone to put the milk bottles out and then just gone for a walk, and forgotten where she lived. A policeman found her sitting on a park bench. I feel dreadful. Anything could have happened to her. He found out where she lived and took her home, but imagine if she did that during the winter. She was only wearing her slippers and her poor feet were so cold.

I have had to put her into a home. I really do feel awful about it. I think she should live with us. I feel as though it is my responsibility to look after her now, as she tried to look after us when we were young. It can't have been easy for her, what with Dad dying and her having to earn money to feed and clothe us. And then she was dead set against my going to London, and you left soon afterwards.

I did think about turning to some of Dad's relatives who live up there and asking them to help out, but then I thought how awful Auntie Beatrice was to us at the funeral and the dreadful things she said about mum being a bit soft in the head. I can't go to her now and hear her say "I told you so" and see her smug look. That would be the ultimate betrayal to mum. Am I wrong? Maybe I am, but it seems I have to make the decisions on my own. James insists that it is the right thing to do, but sometimes I wonder if that is just because he doesn't want her to live with us, and then I hate myself for being disloyal to him.

So, she's in a home and I've been to see her a couple of times. It seems wrong that it should be called a home, as it's nothing like one. There's no love there, only duty. The whole place smells of institutions – you know; boiled cabbage and disinfectant. There are men on the ward who shuffle along with their Zimmer frames and trousers round their ankles and others who drool and look vacant. The doors are always left open 'just in case' and mum's jewellery has mysteriously disappeared. The nurses are efficient but brusque and each time I leave she begs me to take her home.

It must be terrible there for her – she is physically fit, but her mind is really wandering now and she looks lost among all the old people, trapped in some scary nightmare. She asks why I have put her there as though I am punishing her for being naughty and she doesn't know what she has done wrong. I try so hard to be positive when I am there and talk brightly to her, but when I get outside in the car I sit and cry for several minutes before I feel fit to drive home. I don't know whether to take the children or not. She used to love hearing about all their exploits, but now I'm not sure if she would recognise them.

I am enclosing her address, in case you get round to writing to her. She asks about you often. I tell her you are doing well and enjoying life in the sunshine, but what would I know? If you don't write back this time, I'll assume you have moved house or something and there is little point in me continuing to send letters that are unanswered. So I really do hope to hear from you soon and please believe me when I say that I love you as always,

Claire

23rd July '61

Dear Claire,

Wow. I'm sorry I haven't written for a while, but I didn't realise the time had passed. Things are so busy here and there has been so much going on. It sounds really awful about mum, but I'm sure you have done the right thing. You always did know what to do. Thanks for the address, I'll try and write to her when I get some time. Please don't be mad at me, I love getting your letters and am just sorry that I'm not as good at keeping in touch as you are.

We had a Fourth of July party where everyone went down to the beach and just hung out, which was really cool. All these people Hal knows and lots more that he doesn't were there and all these beautiful kids were running around. Dawn was in and out of the water and loads of the guys were looking out for her. We sat around a big camp fire made out of driftwood and passed a few smokes around and just talked about things. A couple of the guys had guitars and we started singing songs and everyone was dancing and it was all just totally beautiful. Most of us slept out under the stars that night, and Dawn curled up under a blanket and fell asleep while the party drifted on around her.

I'm working at the American Embassy, which is allowed because it's on diplomatic soil, so no green card is necessary. I do some typing and filing and help answer the 'phones. The doctors are examining guys to give them their papers for when they get called up. Some of the doctors are pretty decent about the whole thing and they will give a guy a report that says there's something wrong with his lungs or whatever if he objects. Others aren't so understanding and will send guys who disagree with the invasion.

Hal is working on a project at Berkley, the university, and there are lots of talks and sit-ins against the war. Dawn and I go to a lot of them and sing songs and light candles for peace. Dawn looks amazing with her big solemn brown eyes and flowers in her hair and it makes you think why are we killing people when there is so much love in the world? Hal says he doesn't believe in Communism but he doesn't believe in killing either and he doesn't mind that we go to the protests, although he doesn't come with us.

Must go, Hal is coming home soon and he likes dinner ready when he gets in. See, our lives are not so different after all!

Yours in peace,

Jean

12th August, '61

Dear Jean,

Thank you for your letter. At least I know you haven't moved and that you are getting my letters. I'm sorry if I sounded a bit terse with you, but I was worried about mum and needed to know what you thought. You write that I always know what to do. I wish this were true. It is still a struggle each time I go and see her. Now she seems almost resigned to being where she is, and I'm not sure if that isn't somehow worse?

Last time I went to visit, I took Ruth with me. She has dropped out of school and has got a job in a ladies' outfitters. Of course there were fights and tears and recriminations. James and I always wanted to bring our children up to get an education so that they could be independent and do whatever they wanted without having to rely on anyone. I was worried what would happen to her if she didn't pass her exams and I suppose I always imagined they would all go to university and be bright little things. Maybe this was just me pushing my wishes forward at the expense of theirs.

Anyway, Ruth seems to really enjoy her job and has blossomed. She says there a few girls there about her age, and they do the sewing and alterations for the ladies who come in to be measured and fitted for dresses. She had some patterns with her when I took her to see mum, and I popped out to get a pot of tea, and when I returned, they had them spread out all over the bed and were discussing hem lengths and neck lines! I was amazed! I still don't know if mum knew who she was, but it was the most animated I've seen her in months. And Ruth really enjoyed it too. Now that she has found some friends who are interested in the same things she is, she has opened up and become a lot less sullen. She's a delight to be with at the moment.

You write that our lives are not so different, but I can't imagine having wild parties on the beach with all the children running around and falling asleep outside! We did have a party last week for Jennifer's birthday, but it was rather different I'm afraid. I had organised lots of party games like musical chairs and pass the parcel, but I had told Jennifer that she wasn't allowed to win any of the games at her own party, as the little prizes were for the guests. I didn't think she'd mind, but Emma found her crying in the cupboard under the stairs. They'd been playing hide and seek and of course, no one had found her, and they'd moved on to another game without letting her know. I think she felt a bit left out!

In the evening, after all her little friends had gone, I saw the others playing 'pirates' with her in the garden – the one where you have to move about the place without touching the floor. She came in beaming, saying she'd won, and Adam said that she'd been really good at it, but I know that Emma has got much better balance and had to have let her win. My children never cease to amaze me. After she'd gone to bed, I thanked them for being so nice to her and Emma said, 'We couldn't let our little sister cry.' I could have cried myself.

I'm so glad that I have got a little sister of my own and I'm sorry that I got angry with you, but sometimes you feel so far away and I miss you so much.

All my love as always,

Claire

29th September, '61

Dear Jean,

This is just a quick note to let you know that I was thinking about you today. I had a great day with James and the children. We went for a walk through the woods just like old times and picked bucketfuls of blackberries for making pies and jam. Emma and Adam had a sort of competition to see who could get the most and their buckets were soon overflowing. James was asking them how many pounds of fruit went into a jar of jam, and how long did they think it would it take them to collect enough to supply the town grocers. Jennifer followed Ruth around and Ruth helped to reach down the juiciest berries. I don't suspect many made it into the bucket though because Jennifer had purple juice all round her mouth and she complained that she had a bad tummy and went to bed tonight without supper!

James had taken a football and when we reached the clearing, they all put down their pails and kicked it about while I sat and watched. They were arguing about which football players they were and who could score the most goals. I started daydreaming and wished that you could be here with Hal and Dawn; it would have made everything perfect.

Half way down the hill on the way back there is an old tree that overhangs the path and when the children were little they used to run ahead and leap out at us, pretending to be an ambush. Jennifer insisted on doing this, so we had to wait while she went ahead and Ruth had to help her climb the tree. It was so funny because all the leaves had fallen off the tree and she was wearing bright red tights so we could see from a mile away. Then, when she leapt out she knocked her pail of blackberries over, so it was probably a good job there was hardly anything in there. We all had to try really hard not to laugh, and pretend to be surprised, but I think Adam overdid the acting bit when he leapt off the path into a patch of stinging nettles!

We played Pooh Sticks on the way home, and I was pleased that we all got to spend such a pleasant day together. It seems that we don't get to do that very often. I'm enclosing cards from the children and a book for Dawn's birthday – *The Wind in the Willows* which is set around here. I don't know what the scenery is like out there, but these woods are the Wild Woods of the book, so she might like to read all about Ratty and Mole and Badger and Toad and think of her cousins back here, although I'm not sure which one I'm suggesting is which!

Love and miss you as always,

Claire

14th November '61

Dear Claire,

Thanks for Dawn's present and all the cards from the cousins; they were lovely. She's not too big on reading so I hope this gets her into it. I told her how you used to read to me and make up stories when the books ran out. I hope she doesn't go getting any ideas though, because I'm pretty hopeless at all that. She's doing well at school and has a lot of friends, who seem to hang out at each other's houses listening to records and making up dances and little routines. We know most of the parents and have lots of get-togethers with all the moms and dads and kids, when everyone ends up sleeping over and we talk until the early hours of the morning, just falling asleep where we are, but sometimes Hal gets annoyed at the anti-war talk and we leave early.

It was nice to hear your tales of collecting blackberries – you always were good at telling stories. I guess if there's one thing I miss here, it's the seasons. We don't get snow in winter and the trees don't change colour and the leaves fall off like they do back in England. It's pretty much the same all year round, but there's heaps of great fruit. Hal likes the peaches and we buy big bags of them all the time and have them

Mornington Crescent

with ice cream. At the grocers there are piles of plums and nectarines and grapes and they're all really big and perfect. I know that you would bake pies and make jam, but I don't have the patience for all that so we just eat them as is, but you can buy stuff for the freezer which is so cheap that you might as well.

Have you heard of Zinfandel? It's another thing they do really well here, a red wine that's cheap and very tasty. Hal likes it as it makes a change from beer. I reckon you and James would like it, as you used to be keen on the odd glass here and there I seem to remember.

Okay, I better run, love to all,

Jean

17th January '62

Dear Jean,

Happy New Year! We had a nice, relaxing Christmas break, although it felt strange not to have mum here. They said at the home that it was best not to move her as she would be too disorientated, but I went up the week before and there was a Christmas tree with decorations hung up and the nurses told me they would have carol singing and a turkey with all the trimmings which made me feel a little bit less guilty.

My big news is that I have got a job! It's a long story, but I'll cut it short. James got a promotion and so we went to dinner with his colleagues and they were all terribly smart. They were sitting around the table discussing what they did and when they asked what I did, I said I was a mother and they turned their noses up and asked, 'Don't you work?' and 'Don't you get bored?' I thought they had no idea, but I got to thinking about it and I thought, 'I'm as bright as they are and I studied to be a teacher' so I thought that now the children are older and don't need me so much, I would see whether I couldn't get a job.

So I applied for a job at King George's (you know, the local primary school) and I had an interview. I was a little worried because I've not been to anything like that before, but it was fine and they asked me if I would like to start next month! I am going to help out until the end of term and then I'm going to start teaching properly. I'm so excited about it all and James is pleased too. I can't wait to see those smug people now who thought I wasn't worth anything, once I'm earning my own money.

I'm a little bit apprehensive because it's been such a long time since I was around other adults, but I'm sure I can hide in a corner of the staffroom or spend most of my day in the classroom. Imagine – I'll have my very own classroom! I know you'll think this all sounds a bit silly, but it's what I've always wanted!

I have to go and buy some clothes too which is a bit daunting. I have looked in the magazines and all the fashions have changed so much. Ruth says she will take me shopping, which is just so funny – fancy my own daughter telling me what to wear! I trust her judgment though, because she always looks so smart herself and has a wise head on her shoulders. The only thing is, I seem to have put on some weight with all the mince pies and Christmas pudding, so goodness knows what we'll find that will fit.

The children are all doing well. Jennifer has been singing in the school choir and she had her first solo at Christmas. The school performed a carol concert in the local church and she sang 'In the Bleak Mid-Winter'. She looked so cute standing up there by the altar and she was easily the best of all the soloists – not that I'm biased at all! She was nervous beforehand, but afterwards she was floating along on cloud nine and couldn't stop chattering. She says she wants to be a singer on a big stage in

London plays. It's something we won't discourage but I think we'll just see how things go – you know how they change their ideas all the time at this age.

What does Dawn want to be when she grows up? Adam still says he wants to play football and he spends all his time kicking a ball around with his friends. It keeps him out of trouble I suppose. Emma is going to be a vet she tells us and biology is her favourite subject at school. She's actually very good at it and the teachers tell us that if she continues to apply herself, she'll go far. We'll see.

I'm enclosing some photos that we took when we were out walking last month. I never thought that you would miss the trees in all their glory, but then that must be a small price to pay for all that lovely weather.

With lots of love as always,

Claire

27th May '62

Dear Jean,

I'm sorry I haven't written for a while. Things have got really busy here. I have been teaching at the school and I absolutely love it. There's so much to do and prepare for the classes and then feel as though I am really helping to make a difference and teach these children something worthwhile. We have been 'doing the Greeks' and my classroom is covered in pictures of Greek Gods and heroes. We read stories and learn about all sorts of things – many of which I've forgotten so it's fun to rediscover them.

The other teachers are nice. There are a couple that I like and sometimes we go for a coffee after class. One of them has invited us to a party next weekend and I'm ridiculously excited. It's such a long time since I feel as though I've socialised with my own friends. I get a bit frustrated because James seems to belittle it, as though it's just a little thing I do, rather than a proper job. He still expects me to do everything around the home and I do try.

Sometimes I ask the children to help out with the housework or the shopping but I always make sure I pay them for it. I don't give them much, but I don't want them to think that I take them for granted. I don't want them to feel like they have to. I want them to remain children and enjoy things for as long as possible. I don't want life to get too complicated. I always make sure that I am there for them when they get home from school.

Valerie has been helping out quite a lot recently. If I'm going to be a little bit late or if I need to pop out and get something, she will look after the children for me. I think she enjoys being around them, and she talks to them like they are adults rather than little kids, you know how some people do? I think it may even be quite good for them. Of course, there was a bit of a misunderstanding at first because she went to pick Jennifer up from school in her car, and Jennifer wouldn't get in with her. She told her that she wasn't allowed to get into cars with strangers and poor Valerie got really upset, saying that she wasn't a stranger, but Jennifer wouldn't budge. It could have been embarrassing but Valerie laughed it off later. She has become a good friend.

We decided to move mum to a home down here so that we can be closer. I still want to see her as much but I just don't have the time to travel up there so often now. I was worried about moving her from her home town and everything that she knows, but James says that she doesn't really recognise any of it anyway. She has settled in to a new place, which seems much nicer than the last one, and is just over in the next village, only about ten miles away. It is lighter and the rooms seem bigger and more open. I hope you think this is alright. I'm enclosing the new address so that you know where she is.

I was a bit anxious about Adam recently. He loves his football and is always playing in the school team and having matches at weekends and in the evenings, and going to practice. He even washes his own kit and cleans his boots, which is amazing because the rest of his clothes are an absolute mess. I have to peel them off his bedroom floor, and I'm sure the socks could walk to the washing basket on their own! Valerie says she feels lucky that she only had girls, but a couple of the other teachers at school have teenage sons and they say theirs are just as bad. It feels great to have some allies and people to talk to about these things.

Anyway, Adam supports Tottenham Hotspur and he has posters of the team and some of the players on his walls – he tells me that Jimmy Greaves is the best player ever. Spurs made it to the FA Cup Final earlier this month, and he told me that he was going with some of his friends from his own team. He didn't ask me, he told me. I asked James what he thought about this because I was worried – there has been some trouble at matches and they get such huge crowds – there were 100,000 at the match and it was in Wembley which is quite a trip for a young lad. James said that he wasn't a young lad anymore and that I shouldn't try to keep him tied to my apron strings. So eventually I relented and let him go.

I know he's a sensible boy and there was no trouble. Spurs won 3-1 against Burnley (I think, it was one of those northern teams), so that must have helped the situation. I don't know what would have happened if I had said he couldn't go. I suspect he probably would have done anyway. I marvel at how they grow up so fast and become independent people. It feels like only yesterday that I held him in my arms and James and I were amazed at the wonder of twins.

Adam brought the programme home and I caught him showing it to Jennifer. He teaches her all the moves and the players' names and nick-names. She follows his side although I think that's more to do with the fact that she worships her big brother than that she appreciates the team. I think she likes the ritual of it, with everyone having their own position and their own job, and she sings all the songs and the chants that he teaches her. I've never heard any bad language, so I'm sure he must shield her from those songs, as I'm positive they must have them. He is a good boy and I know I can trust him, but I don't think you ever stop worrying, do you? Once a mother, always a mother and all that.

Goodness, I've just realised the time. I must go and do the hoovering. I have to get it done before James gets home, because he hates the sound and says it disturbs him. I know it sounds silly, but I want to prove that just because I have got a job, it doesn't mean I am neglecting the home, or the children. I want him to be proud of me and have no reason to find fault. I must say, Jean, that these days I am pretty tired with all this extra work, but I am so happy. I had almost forgotten what a thrill it was to teach. Don't get me wrong, I know I do an important job at home, but at last I feel as though I might be making a difference!

Love to you all as always,

Claire

July 12th '62

Dear Claire,

Well congratulations on your job, and good for you! It sounds as though it's just what you needed and I'm really happy for you. You'll get to meet all sorts of people now and get out and about. I don't know how I would have coped if I'd been cooped up in the house with four children all the time, but you always were so capable. Even as a child I used to feel overshadowed by you, you were always the good one and I just sort of muddled along. I know that James has a high-powered job and is very clever, but you mustn't put yourself down or let him do it to you. You are a wonderful woman.

Would you listen to me? I have joined an encounter group, as you may be able to tell when I come out with all of that empowerment talk. There are a dozen of us and we meet at a local hall and discuss our feelings in a safe and non-threatening environment. We don't have to play nice or obey society's rules and things can get a little bit wacky. We rant and rave and say things that we never would normally, and then we all shuffle off home to our own lives, feeling much better for having gotten it all off our chests. Of course Hal doesn't come because he doesn't like talking about emotions but that's fine. It may not be everybody's bag, but it sure works for me!

I had good reason to be angry last week. We were having our July Fourth celebrations and it started raining late in the evening. It has been so hot here that everyone has just about been going crazy so it was a real relief. Dawn and a couple of her friends stripped off and started dancing around in the garden. They were just messing about, spinning with their arms out wide and catching raindrops on their tongues. The rain was warm and they weren't doing any harm, so we left them to it.

Anyway, the next thing I know, the police are at the front door because someone has reported that there is an obscenity going on in our garden! Some neighbour, and I'm pretty sure I know who, had phoned them up and complained, like there was some sort of an orgy or something. It was on our property anyway, so I don't see how it was anyone else's business, and they're just kids. Who cares if they want to run around naked and enjoy their bodies? I told the cop that I didn't see what was obscene about the human body and he was pretty embarrassed but he said he had to act on the complaint.

Nothing came of it but Hal was furious that we'd had the cops to our house, where they might have found all sorts of things if they'd looked, and he yelled at Dawn and sent her friends home. So now she's not speaking to him and I'm caught in the middle, although I am on her side. Sometimes he's just such a prude, but I can't get through to him and he says it's his house and she'll obey his rules while she lives there. Sometimes he makes me so

mad, there's simply no arguing with him! Anyway, thank god for the encounter group, right? I can scream my head off there if I want to!
Love

Jean

8th September '62

Dear Jean,

I've just come home from a really tough visit to see mum. She didn't know who I was and kept asking where baby Jean was. I tried to tell her that you were in America but she got all confused and couldn't understand why you were there when you were only a little girl. Then she asked me why Albert hadn't been to see her for a while and without thinking I said that he had died.

Well, that set her off into floods of tears and she kept asking when and how and why hadn't anybody told her. I didn't know which was worse – the fact that she had forgotten, or that I had broken her heart all over again with the news. She lay down on her bed and turned her face to the wall and just sobbed. There was nothing I could say or do. She started fretting about the funeral arrangements, but I told her it had all been taken care of. She wanted to know what hymns had been sung and why she wasn't there.

I must admit, I felt scared. Whatever happens, your mum is meant to be there for you – the strong one, and now it feels as though she's gone. She looks the same, but old, but her memory has gone and I don't know whether it is better to try and refresh it, or just to pretend. I wonder if she will remember that Dad is dead next time, or whether I will have to tell her again. It's not easy for me, having to talk about dad dying either. I asked one of the nurses and she says they generally just stick to easy topics and don't mind if the patients repeat themselves over and over again. I can't ignore her if she asks questions, though, she gets so upset and she looks at me as though I have let her down. I think she is scared as she doesn't know what she doesn't know, if that makes any sense.

School term has just started again and I have lots of new children to teach. One of them called me mummy by accident in class today and it made me want to cry. My own don't call me that any more – it is far too babyish for them. I hope they never end up having to look after me. I hope I see them all grow up before I die. I hope they will all be okay. And you and Dawn – I think about you a lot too and I just wish there was a way we could keep them from suffering. I don't know how you teach love.

With all my love as always,

Claire

October 2nd '62

Dear Claire,

Thank you for your last letter, although you sounded so sad. I know I am far away but I do think of you often and I really appreciate the fact that you, as always, are looking after everything. Gee, I find it so tough sometimes looking after my little family, and there's only the three of us. I don't know how you cope – you are a marvel.

I know you're sad about mom, but I think you have to let go a little. We all get old, and maybe if her mind has gone, that isn't such a bad thing. She was never really a momsy-type mom was she? So, maybe now you guys can play a little and do all the stuff we could never do when we were young. Maybe you could just brush her hair or do her nails or just go for walks with her – we never did that. I remember her being fierce and strong but often absent. I know it must be tough, but life can be beautiful if you look for the little things.

And relax. You don't have to be super-mom. You are already – your kids are great, and you are super-daughter, and super-sister. I bet you're super-teacher too and I'm not surprised those kids at school call you mummy – you're just so good at taking care of people, and so giving. I never worry about getting old or Dawn's future, because

I know that you would always do everything for her if anything happened to me. And I guess I've never said it, but I will always help your lot in any way I can – you should know that.

Maybe you could learn to take care of yourself a little though, because you are a very special person. You have gotten yourself a great job. Try to enjoy it and stop worrying about everyone else. I have been going to yoga classes, which I find are great for relaxation. At the end of the class they leave us with a message, and today's was

"All shall be well, and all shall be well, and all manner of things shall be well."

I think it's from the Bible and I'm not into religion at all – you know your Bible much better than me – but I found it comforting.

Lots of love,

Jean

31st October '62

Dear Jean,

Thank you so much for your last letter; it was nice and cheerful and made me feel a lot better. I'm sorry that I must often seem to be moaning in my letters, but that's just because you're my sister and if I can't tell you, who can I tell? Anyway, it was lovely to hear from you and to see that you are busy exploring new things. I had to ask someone at school what yoga was, and she told me it was all about bending and stretching and breathing techniques, which sounds wonderful, but I'm not sure I could get into any of those positions – and if I did, I might not ever be able to get up again!

I did take your other advice, however, and I spent a great day with mum last weekend. We played, which felt strange but good. I didn't treat her like a child, because I hate it when some of the nurses do that, but we went for a walk and sat on a bench and tried to guess the names of the plants and trees in the garden. She never really taught us much about any of that stuff, did she, and I certainly haven't learned many as I haven't got much time to do any gardening.

We collected some leaves that had fallen and there was a book in the little library about identifying trees so we looked at oaks and sycamores and beech trees and all sorts. I think I might do a couple of lessons about trees in my class at school and get the children to gather leaves from different trees and make pictures – they're such pretty colours in autumn. It's also really interesting to see all the different nuts like acorns and sycamore wings and pine cones, and I thought maybe we can have a conker tournament at school.

Mum and I started talking about all this and she got really enthusiastic about it all. She remembered the proverbs, "Mighty oak trees from little acorns grow" and "Every majestic oak tree was once a nut who stood his ground". I've never heard that one before and I wonder how she can dredge things like that from her memory and yet forget the details of her personal life. Maybe it's because she used to be a writer and her mind is full of all sorts of scraps of information. But I decided not to let it bother me because she was happy.

We talked about historical incidents to do with trees and forests, like Robin Hood, yew trees in churchyards and willow in cricket bats. We went on to think of place names with trees in them like Royal Oak, Sevenoaks, Aintree, and she says there is a place in New Zealand called One Tree Hill where she would like to go one day. I don't think there's much chance of that, but her eyes lit up as she started going off on tangents and I had to write down half of her ideas to use at school, or I would have forgotten them all!

Jennifer has just come prancing into the kitchen in her Halloween outfit. She has been learning about witches and goblins and goodness knows what else at her school. She doesn't seem frightened by any of it, because she says they should be allowed a day to wander about before All Saints Day when she will remember all the good people. She said she wanted to play at being naughty for a day too, but she promised to only be 'a little bit naughty' which was really sweet. Her idea of naughty is to have apple bobbing and to hang apples from pieces of string from the ceiling and try and bite them with her hands behind her back. I suppose if that's her idea of mischief, things can't be too bad.

She has bossed us all about and we have all got jobs to do. Emma is helping her to carve out a gap-toothed grinning face on a turnip for the jack-o-lantern, Adam is preparing the games, I am going to make the toffee apples, and Ruth has made her the most amazing little witch costume. It is made out of black and purple velvet, strung with bits of netting to look like cobwebs, and she has even got a pointy hat and a wand. Ruth is amazingly clever with what she can do and so patient. She takes all the measurements and spends ages working out the design and thinking about the fabric, and then she runs it up in no time at all.

She came home from work the other day and said she has been offered a position as an apprentice with a fashion designer who has been into the shop several times and admires her ability and flair. I am worried about her taking it because it is such a grown up world, but she says it is a great opportunity and she would be mad to pass it up. Once again, I have to remember not to hold them back and to accept that they must make their own adventures, but of course I am scared for her. She is going to have a trial for a month up to Christmas and see how it goes. I have to admit, that underneath the worry, I am bursting with pride for her, and really hope that it works out.

Now I really must go, as Jennifer is clamouring for me to move my things so she can get carving on the kitchen table!

Love as always,

Claire

12th November '62

Dear Jean,

I thought I would write to you after speaking on the phone, but I don't know what to say. I find it hard to believe that mum is dead. She seemed so happy the last time I saw her and her mind was more alive than it has been in ages. I take some comfort from the thought that she may even have recognised me, and she certainly mentioned you, as she did on every visit, asking after little Jean.

I have been taking care of the funeral arrangements and have been given time off work to sort things out. I took out a notice in the paper, which I am enclosing – I hope I did the right thing and you approve of the words. I understand that you can't make it. I know it is a long way to come. The nurses at the home have been wonderful and they are very helpful. Although I suppose they are used to this sort of thing in their line of work, they are still very compassionate.

I am thinking of you and I miss you so much. There aren't many of us left now, are there?

I love you,

Claire

November 12th '62

Dear Claire,

Thank you for phoning me yesterday. I know it was late and the line was terrible, but I'm glad you called me at once. I am so sorry to hear that mom has died. I am also sorry that I won't be able to make it over for the funeral. Does it cost much money? We can send whatever you need. I feel for you dealing with everything. I wouldn't even know where to start or what to do.

I know I have never believed in religion as you have, but I do think there is something somewhere that holds it all together and maybe mom will be joining dad there now. I know she loved him more than anything and has missed him since he died. If her memory went, then perhaps this is a relief and the best thing for everyone. I would like to remember her as the slightly odd and scary woman who wrote stories we never read, shooed us out of the house from under her feet and stood up to everyone.

I know she did the best she could for us, and you're right, it must have been hard for her after Dad died, but somehow I feel as though I never really knew her.

I never actually talked to her and I just sort of felt as though you were more of a mother to me than she was. I'm glad she's at peace and I hope you can start to live your own life now.

Lots of love,

Jean

20th November, '62

Dear Jean,

Mum's funeral went off well. We made a decent little group; James and me and the children, and some of the nurses from the home. Someone from her publishers came as a mark of respect, which was nice, and there was one woman who sat at the back of the church. When I asked her to come for tea afterwards she said she didn't want to intrude, but she was a great fan of mum's work. That made me smile to think that mum had a fan and that all her writing had made people happy who we don't even know.

And guess who came? Well, you won't be able to, so I'll tell you. Lizzie (only she calls herself Liz now) and Eddie. Do you remember they're sort of mum's cousins from down on the coast and I stayed with them during the war when we were evacuated? I couldn't believe how good it was to see them! Liz is married but she and her husband and children still live on the farm with Eleanor – there's lots of space and they've built a separate little house for Eleanor to move into. She said she was sorry for losing touch – although it's as much my fault – and promised to do so more in future. I hope we do, I'd forgotten how lovely she is.

As for Eddie, well I never told you this, but Eddie and I had a bit of a thing together all those years ago, and we've not seen each other since. I felt really awkward at seeing him again and started blushing like a fool, especially when he said he was divorced, which made me feel really stupid. He's given up his share of the farm and works for the Royal National Lifeboat Institution, which I'm pleased about as he was always keen on the sea and saving souls. He and Liz had to get away but it was lovely to see them again. Anyway, he seemed as nice and relaxed as ever, and James was completely oblivious when I introduced them. Of course, there's no reason why he shouldn't be, and it's ridiculous to be embarrassed about something that happened so long ago, but memories are strange things, aren't they? Sometimes even a nice memory can be so strong it's almost like a physical pain, don't you think?

The biggest surprise of the day, though, was Aunty Beatrice. I was shocked to see her there, as I had always though she hated mum, but it turns out she had always just been concerned for her brother and then for our welfare. (Let's face it, mum could give the impression of being neglectful). She apologised for making a scene and upsetting me all those years ago at Dad's funeral. She said she knew she had handled the situation badly but had never stopped thinking of us. She asked after you and seemed pleasantly amused to hear that you were in America. Just think, all these years I'd cast her as the wicked witch, but really she's just a pragmatic woman who was trying to do the best for a couple of girls she hardly knew, even if she went about it all the wrong way. Isn't it funny how coming together for a death or a funeral can sometimes be the start of a new beginning? Let's hope so anyway.

Jennifer sang 'Abide with Me' which was beautiful, especially the last verse. I cried at the words, "Hold thou thy cross before my closing eyes; Shine through the gloom and point me to the skies. Heaven's morning breaks and earth's vain shadows flee; in life, in death, O Lord, abide with me." I hope you're right. I hope she is at peace now. We all sang 'The Lord is My Shepherd' which had always been her favourite, and I hope he is looking after her now, wherever she may be. When the vicar read out the bit about there being many rooms in my father's house, one of the nurses said, "Yes, and I bet she's making sure he's cleaning it and making the beds properly too!" I had to laugh because she obviously terrorised the nurses too, although they spoke of her affectionately and she clearly meant enough to them for them to come to her funeral. I let them take the flowers away to the home, so they can brighten up the place – the living will appreciate them more than the dead.

We had loads of sandwiches that I had made, but there was no one to eat them. I don't know what I had been thinking. I had sat up until late the night before with Jennifer, cutting them into perfect little triangles. James said I should save them and we could have them for lunches, but I couldn't bear the thought, so I threw them all away, which I suppose was rather wasteful. Adam drank too much sherry and was sick in the flowerbed. I pretended not to notice. I didn't have the heart to tell him off and besides, what does it matter?

I remembered Dad's funeral and how I poured the endless cups of tea. Suddenly I couldn't stand it any longer and I smashed the teapot on the floor. I don't know what came over me, but I just couldn't take one more cup of hot sweet sympathy. Ruth came to give me a hug and Emma swept up the pieces. They acted as though it was nothing, and James took Jennifer away so she wouldn't see her family falling apart. I think I saw it all repeating all over again and I promised them I would always be their mother and never their dependant. I hope it's a promise I can keep.

This morning when I came down to breakfast, I found Adam already up and making it. He was guilty for last night and he apologised over and over again. He told me he would never drink again but I said of course he would, and I remember saying the same thing myself once. He looked shocked as though he can't ever imagine me having been young and fun. Have I always been old?

Emma came down, asked who wanted tea and went to make a pot. When she remembered, she stopped in her tracks. Ruth said we needed a new one anyway and she was going to buy one this afternoon. James gave me a big hug and said he always drank coffee at work and why didn't we try that at home? Of course, we didn't have any, so he said we should go out to a coffeehouse. We all piled into the car and went for a drive out to a café which was really quite pleasant. I felt that I shouldn't be enjoying myself the day after my mother's funeral, but when I looked around at my wonderful family, I just couldn't help it.

Love as always,

Claire

10th Jan '63

Dear Claire,

How are you guys? I'm glad mum's funeral was bearable – I was thinking of you and knew you'd manage it with your usual style. What amazing news about Aunty Beatrice – it's great that she showed up for mum, and you of course. I'd never have thought it after all these years of thinking of her as such a villain. Children see things so differently – I guess as we get older we realize things aren't so black and white, although sometimes it would be easier if they were.

And how about Eddie, you dark horse! Fancy you and some long-lost cousin having a fling! I'm terribly hurt that you didn't tell me about it at the time! Seriously, it sounds like he provided a bright spark in an otherwise gloomy day. I laughed at the thought of you blushing over some romantic incident that happened a million years ago. Give yourself a break – you deserve a little fun and frivolity. Of course you won't do anything about it (although a little innocent flirtation isn't always a bad thing), but a little tingle can make you feel alive, and don't worry about James – we all need a secret or two – as long as they're harmless!

Thanks also for the Christmas presents – the scarves are beautiful, and we got some great use out of them on our holidays! We went to Lake Tahoe over the school break and had a great time. We went skiing at Squaw Valley, which is where they held the winter Olympics a couple of years back.

Hal just loved swishing down the slopes – and drinking some spicy rum drink afterwards! He got talking to everyone and pretty soon we were spending all our evenings touring round other people's little chalets. Dawn wasn't so keen on the skiing – she kept falling over. I don't think balance is her strong point. Then she would get really cross and grouchy and whine, saying she hated the snow because it made her wet and cold. We dined out in the restaurants and I think she liked that a lot better. She discovered the best hot chocolate which certainly seemed to keep her happy.

I loved the skiing. I wasn't any good at it and didn't have the technique that Hal seems to take for granted, but I just loved being out there in the snow, on top of the mountains. It's so beautiful and can be real quiet and peaceful. The air is so clear – you feel at one with nature and as though your mind is being emptied of all negative energy and just filled with calm and purity. I can't really explain, but it felt just great. It made me realize that we live in such a wonderful world.

Maybe it was just nice to get away. Hal is so busy at work; there is heaps of building going on, and the students are getting more and more agitated. This war is bothering everyone and it's hard to relax. Everyone has an opinion and you daren't express your thoughts for fear of getting into an argument and upsetting someone. Hal has mentioned that his company might be sending him to Vietnam to build some army stuff for the boys out there. I sure hope it doesn't come to anything. We keep sending them out, but not so many are coming back.

Lots of love,

Jean

26th February '63

Dear Jean,

I bought you this postcard of London today. It is half term and I went up to go to an exhibition at an art gallery, but as I was walking along the banks of the Thames, I just stopped and sat there thinking, even though it was bitterly cold. I think London is beautiful. I know it is a mess, with buildings right next to each other from all different eras and lots of higgledy-piggledy designs, but it is a working city and it's not as formal or imposing as some others. And the history is amazing and so resilient. It feels like a person – embattled but not beaten. I find it incredible to think that it was bombed to rubble and yet has emerged with such strength and power. I agree that we live in a wonderful world and there is beauty in humanity. I have faith that this humanity will see us all through. I hope the war is over soon. We've seen enough of fighting and death.

All my love as always,

Claire

15th March '63

Dear Claire

Okay, now don't panic, but I've got some news, and it's not good. I don't really know how to tell you this, so I'll just come out and say it. I have been diagnosed with cancer. Hal found a lump on my breast and he said it hadn't always been there, so I went and got it checked out, and it's malignant. I don't know how or why it's happened. The doctors said it could be one of any number of things. I guess it doesn't matter – all that matters now is that I beat this thing.

I have been given lots of drugs and I have to have chemotherapy. It's not pleasant and there's a whole heap of side effects, but mainly I feel tired and sick and don't want to eat anything. Hal is great because he doesn't get alarmed by anything and he is very practical. I have told Dawn that I am sick and I have caught a disease, but I don't want to frighten her. This is pretty difficult, because I am scared myself. But Hal and the doctors say there is a lot of hope for me because I am young and strong, so we will see. I have had to give up work because I feel too sick, but Hal is working hard and there is enough money for us all to live on quite comfortably.

I guess I'm going to have to take each day as it comes for a while and trust in what you said about the wonderful world and the beautiful humanity. I must admit, at times it is pretty hard to see it. Please don't worry – there is nothing you can do, and I will fight this. I just thought you should know.

Love

Jean

1ˢᵗ April '63

My dearest Jean,

I have just written the date and how I wish your letter had been an April Fool. I know that this isn't some kind of sick joke, though this will have a happy ending, you must believe that. I'm sorry I got so upset on the telephone – I know that won't help anyone and I promise not to again. Of course I am upset by this news – you are my sister and I feel everything you feel – but you are right – you are young and strong, and you will beat this.

The medication sounds awful and I hate to think of you being sick. You must rest and let Hal look after you. I know you always want to rush around experiencing things, but just rest for a while. If there is anything at all that I can do for you, I will do it. You know that. I know you said you wanted me to just act as normally as possible and so I will try. I have discussed it with James and we have not told the children, so please don't think that they are being insensitive if they don't mention anything.

I am sending a couple of books that I have read recently and enjoyed. *Cider With Rosie*, *Mrs. 'Arris Goes to Paris*, and *The Prime of Miss Jean Brodie*. They are all very good in very different ways and gave me lots to think about. I imagined reading them to you, and I hope they force you to sit still as I know that will be quite a difficult task for you!

Did I tell you we did that project at school with the leaves and the trees that I had talked about with mum? We made a huge picture of a tree which decorated the classroom and all the children helped to colour it in showing the different seasons. At parents evening, all the parents admired it and said that their children had loved the project and could tell them all about trees now when they went out for walks in the countryside. I was so pleased, and when the headmaster called me into his office to tell me that he had received a great response from parents too, I felt as though we had done something worthwhile, and that maybe mum had managed to help out a little bit. This might sound silly, I know, but I felt she approved.

All my love, always,

Claire

7th May '63

Dear Jean,

I've noticed a lot of young girls here are wearing these turban type things these days. It's very fashionable on the streets of London, so I'm told. As an old married woman, I wouldn't know such things, but Ruth tells me it's true so it must be – she is the absolute authority on such matters. So, I hope you don't mind, but I thought I'd send you this emerald green one, which I can imagine suiting your colouring beautifully. Remember how you used to struggle to get the school beret to sit on your curls? At least that's one thing you won't have to worry about now! I really am not making light of it, it must be so awful for you to lose your hair, but I hope you'll find this latest fashion trend useful.

Ruth is still working for the fashion designer in London who is very pleased with her and has taken her on full-time. She is boarding there now and the family she stays with during the week is very nice and look after her very well. We went to meet them and all went out for a meal together. Ruth loves it there and her wages have increased, so she has a bit of money to spend. She says she gets some input into the collections and all the clothes that she wants. Some of the skirts and dresses are very short, and the shoes are certainly different, but she always looks immaculate. She has such a confidence now, I wish you could see her – she's a different person from last year. James says some of the prints she wears give him a headache, but I tell him to be quiet. She comes down to us every weekend and we should be grateful, no matter what she chooses to wear.

Adam is still football crazy and heads away every other weekend following his team. He still plays for a local team and sometimes they go to the pub for a couple of beers after matches. He is so grown up! He has overtaken James in skill and fitness, but James won't hear any of it. He doesn't go to watch Adam play, because Adam has asked him not to, which I think is rather sad. Adam says he criticises too much and puts him off, but James says he is only trying to help. They argue a lot, but I suppose that's to be expected at their age – both of them are as stubborn as each other. As Valerie says, boys will be boys, no matter what age they are!

Emma is doing really well at school and is so serious. She spends a lot of her time round at her friend's farm, where they have horses. Fortunately, she doesn't seem to want a horse of her own, but she knows all about them and helps her friend look after them. She has also taken to helping out at the vet – she cleans the cages and the surgery and makes sure the animals that have to stay in have enough to eat. I think she may be serious about this vet thing, after all.

Jennifer is still not serious about anything, which I think is lovely. Why should she have to make decisions so young? She is happy singing in the choir and performing in school plays. She is also taking drama classes, which she says she enjoys, but this may be just because they clash with Brownies, and I don't think she was ever keen on that. She used to laugh at dancing round the toadstool and could never tie knots properly. Why did she need to learn that? I don't think I've ever tied a knot in my life! Mind you, making her bed and cleaning her shoes wouldn't go amiss now and then. Did we learn that at Brownies, or was it just something we always did?

Anyway, I hope you are well and recovering from your latest bout of chemotherapy. Please let me know if there's anything at all that I can do to help, and know that I am thinking of you.

With all my love as always,

Claire

2nd June '63

Dear Claire,

Thank you for the turban. I wear it out to cover my baldness. It is so strange having no hair after all those years of complaining about my curls. If I had my time over, I would never bitch about that again. I am learning to be grateful for so many things. Dawn doesn't like the turban, I'm afraid. She says it makes me look like a wicked old witch. This thing is frightening enough as it is. I don't want to scare her any more.

The drugs seem to be working a little and apparently I am in remission. I still feel very weak, but at least I am not vomiting so much. Honestly, the human body can be pretty gross at times!

As I said before, I am learning to be positive. There is so much to enjoy in life. I don't go to those groups anymore because they seem to be full of rage and that is the last thing I need these days. I guess I have had a chance to see what people mean to me and to let them know, so I can say to them that I love them and hold my daughter and smell her hair and appreciate how wonderful this all is. I wish I had the chance to talk to mom properly, but at least I can talk to my own daughter and tell her how much I love her, so if I die, she will always know that.

I want you to know it too. It's odd to think that I am able to say whatever I want, a chance to set my life in order, and I don't know what to say. I have little to give anyone, and less to leave. I guess I just don't know what to say, except thank you for being such a great sister. You gave me a lot of courage and showed me how things could be done. You looked after me all through my childhood and helped me become the person I am today. Well, maybe not today, but you know what I mean. I am so grateful and I admire you so much. You have a wonderful family and you have kept that together through everything. You are the best big sister anyone could ever have.

It's a weird feeling not knowing what may happen, but I'm okay with it. I take each day as it comes. Some are better than others. Hal is being great. He has put his work on hold, and there is no more talk of him going to Vietnam at the moment. I feel he is restless and he goes for long walks. I can't walk very far or fast at the moment, but I do my yoga and that helps. I am at peace with myself.

Love and kisses,

Jean

18th July '63

Dear Jean,

It is the summer holidays now so the children are at home, apart from Ruth. Adam must now wait for the results of his exams to see what he is going to do. He is anxious as he wants to go to university to study architecture of all things. I don't really know where this has come from, but it is a new passion. A teacher at his school is taking the football team on a tour of Italy to play various teams over there. They are going for four weeks and I don't know if he is more interested in the football or the ruins! James says he will be more interested in the women, but I don't think about such things – he's my little boy! He is walking around the house muttering Italian phrases that he's been learning, and what with Jennifer singing bits of opera and Emma insisting that I make some pasta dishes for dinner, we're feeling quite cosmopolitan.

I think I might ask him to bring back as much information as possible and maybe I can use it in my classes when we do Roman civilization – we did the Greeks last year. I still love teaching. I learn all sorts of new things and share them with the class. They seem to know when you're really enthusiastic or just going through the motions. I'm so glad I applied for this job. I love the countries best – I always did like geography at school, and history; learning about people and places that were far away from us. I suppose I always wanted to travel, and you were the one who did it.

Thank you so much for your last letter. It means a lot to me to know that you admire me. I always tried to do the right thing, but I never knew if I had succeeded. I think my life is very dull compared with yours – all the things you have done and all the places you have seen. But please don't think in the past tense. So many things are still out there waiting to be discovered, and you are the person to do it! Of course I love you too. I would say it goes without saying, but I will say it anyway.

All my love as always,

Claire

30th July '63

Dear Jean,

How are you? I hope you are well. I'm glad to hear that you have stopped being sick – it must be a terrible feeling. The body can be awful, can't it, but it is also amazingly resilient, which is a good thing!

The house is empty today and I'm not used to the quiet. James is working in his study. He's doing the correspondence and I know better than to interrupt him. Adam has gone away to Italy. I had a breathless phone call from Rome before he was cut off. He sounds so excited and says he has sent us a postcard already. He's a good boy really.

Ruth is so busy with her work; she is such a young lady these days and I think she may have a boyfriend because she blushes when she mentions a certain name. I don't want to ask too many questions, but I really hope she feels she can confide in me. I don't want her to make the mistakes I made when I was younger, but I suppose heartache is something we must each discover for ourselves.

Emma is working at the vets. She came top in her biology and brought home glowing reports from her teachers. She loves all the animals and she studies hard. I think she means business. Jennifer is practicing with the choir. She sings in church now, and I love to hear it, but James doesn't go because he says it's all too religious.

So the house is quiet and I feel strangely alone. I know there are a million things I should be doing, but I don't know where to start, and the prospect of washing and ironing and cooking and cleaning doesn't thrill me, so I thought I'd sit and write to you. And now I find that I have nothing to write about. Does my life really revolve around the children so much? I suppose it does. And I love my family, I really do, but I wonder what will happen when they don't need me?

Right, that's enough of that. Listen to me! It's a beautiful sunny day and I don't know what to do with it. Now that I have my husband to myself for once, I shall drag him away from his boring old bills and make him take me for a walk to the park and buy me an ice cream! You're right; the simple pleasures in life are the best!

All my love,

Claire

15th August '63

Dear Claire,

It's come back – the drugs haven't worked. I have been given a wheelchair because I am too weak to walk. The doctor says I haven't got long. I am so scared. I don't want to die. I'm not ready. Please come.

Jean

PART FOUR

1

Ruislip

Zone 6: Metropolitan and Piccadilly (between Ickenham and Ruislip Manor).

Nearby attractions: London Swing Dance Society; Polish War Memorial; Ruislip Lido Railway.

Ruislip Lido is a sandy beach by a reservoir, which was originally built to feed the Grand Union Canal. It was used for skating when frozen in the 1920s winters and swimming and boating in the summer. People from all over London flocked to it in the 1960s and 70s for paddle boats, a miniature railway, crazy golf, and the world waterskiing championships. It was the setting for the sinking of Titanic in the film A Night to Remember.

In the 1970s, the council increased admission charges and succeeded only in killing the golden goose. Retailers and traders, no longer able to afford the rents, packed up and left. A final attempt at coaxing people back was made when a chess set with two-foot pieces was introduced, but these were soon thrown into the lake where they took their chances with the Canada geese.

With no attractions, people stopped coming.

According to local legend, a National Nature Reserve, intriguingly named Mad Bess Wood, owes its name to the demented wife of a gamekeeper who prowled the woods at night looking for poachers. It is part of the Ruislip Woods and is dissected by the Hillingdon Trail.

****

'Everything alright?'

James reaches out his arms as Claire slips off her dressing gown and comes back to bed. She snuggles against his warmth and he encircles her with strength and safety. He murmurs slightly as she wriggles her cold bottom into the warm groove of his stomach but he doesn't complain. He knows how hard this is for her. She has trouble sleeping now and she often gets up to check on the children and to sob quietly, trying not to disturb anyone. She smiles bravely but he sees the rings around her eyes; the hollows on her cheeks. He tries to make her feel less alone, but he knows she feels like the sole survivor and like sole survivors everywhere, she suffers guilt. He has heard her whispering, 'Why me?' and he knows she is going through the motions for them, to be strong for her family, but he wants her to do it for herself. The family is strong enough.

She told him some of the horrors. She told him of the extra soft toothbrush she bought because Jean's mouth was full of sores. She told him of the catheter bag she emptied and how she became adept at analysis of the colour yellow, through pale straw to dark brown. She told him how they had to move Jean to prevent the bed sores, but when they moved her she had seizures. She told him how the wheelchair sat in the middle of the room, a silent sentinel begging to be used, but even that was beyond her. She told him how Hal had turned away from physical weakness and taken to exercise, as if by punishing his body with weights and resistance, he could remove some of Jean's pain and sickness. She told him how she had slept on the floor beside her sister so she would be ready to lift the cup of water to her lips. She told him how she looked so old and then young again when she finally died.

He knows she goes to church. He doesn't know she sits and feels nothing. That she is too scared to ask whether there is something out there, and if there is, why did this happen. Why do good people die? He doesn't know that her ideals of life are confused, and she questions whether there is any point to anything. He doesn't know she is scared of her own anger.

They didn't bury the body. They scattered the ashes in the mountains. There was no funeral; no speeches; no flowers; no grand finale. There is nowhere to visit; nowhere to sit and talk quietly; nowhere to lay wreaths and pay respects. It is the Lakota way. It is not her way. Jean is nowhere now. And she is everywhere. And Claire doesn't know what to think, or how to feel.

She wants to protect Dawn. But Dawn is far away with her father and is getting on with life. She is back at school and has friends and boyfriends. They develop so fast over there. Dawn doesn't tell her anything. She writes infrequently and is rarely at home when Claire calls to try and speak to her down the crackling echoing line. She hears her own voice ringing in her ears as the echo bounces back from the void. She wonders, is there an echo in a vacuum? She knows she could ask James, but she doesn't really want to know. She can't think about the vacuum without feeling herself spinning away into space and she is trying so hard to keep her feet on the ground. James suggested she see a doctor, but she told him she can't take pills to remove her grief. She has lost faith in doctors. She has lost faith in drugs. She has lost faith.

Kennedy is shot. The Beatles tour America. Dawn phones to ask if she has ever met them. The styles that Ruth helps to create explode onto the catwalk in a riot of youth and dissatisfaction. Fashion is everything and London is the place to be. Adam passes all his exams and goes to study art history at university. It is cold. Claire is numb. She feels like the world is freezing.

2

Marble Arch

Zone 1: Central, between Lancaster Gate and Bond Street.

Nearby attractions: Hyde Park; Marble Arch; Speakers' Corner; Tyburn Convent.

Marble Arch is, unsurprisingly, a marble arch which is, quite surprisingly, in the middle of a roundabout. It was originally built as the triumphal gateway to Buckingham Palace, but was moved to its present location in 1851 when the palace was extended.

Now it sits almost opposite Speakers' Corner in Hyde Park where anyone who wants to can address the public and share their views. A number of eclectic personages have taken up this very English tradition of eccentric expressionism including Karl Marx, Frederick Engels, Vladimir Lenin, William Morris, George Orwell, and a million tourists.

As anyone from any class or culture may attend and debate, it is a symbol of true democracy. It is considered to be a bastion of free speech as anyone can turn up unannounced and speak about anything they like: the police will not interfere – unless there is profanity, violence or complaints – although those who pontificate are likely to get heckled.

In less permissive times, the nearby Tyburn Tree was actually the King's Gallows, a particular arrangement that allowed for mass-hangings. These were a hugely popular form of entertainment and attended by large crowds – London apprentices were given the day off to join in the fun. For a fee people could see the public executions from a spectator stand, although on one occasion a stand collapsed, killing and injuring hundreds of 'innocent' people.

The last hanging here was of a highwayman, John Austin, in 1783. The gallows are commemorated by three brass triangles in the middle of Edgware Road, and a shrine at the Tyburn Convent (a cloistered monastery in the centre of London) dedicated to the memory of the martyrs executed there.

****

Claire shades the sun from her eyes and watches as Jennifer runs around the square chasing the pigeons. She pauses to pat the lions before continuing her circuit flapping her arms and startling the birds as much as the tourists with their maps and backpacks.

She flops down beside Claire, panting unnecessarily and rests her head on her shoulder.

'Idiot child' Claire says, fondly. 'Have you quite finished?'

'Hmm, for now.' Jennifer grins and laughs. 'They'll still be here next time!'

Every time she comes to London she insists on visiting Nelson and his bronze guardians, and although she is 26, she still hasn't got over the thrill of chasing the pigeons. She sighs and turns to look at her mother with a stern expression.

'Right. Now which way?'

'Well, you've got the map.'

'Oh yes, so I have.' Jennifer pulls a crumpled piece of paper from her pocket and smoothes it out. Claire rolls her eyes and tuts loudly. It was Jennifer's idea that they walk around London to find the gallery, rather than take the tube. 'It's a beautiful day!' she had insisted, and persuaded her mother that she didn't want to be stuck down underground today, when they had time to roam. The problem is she's only got a tube map and has been trying to navigate by that.

So far they have been back and forth along the river, crossing bridges all over the place and walking for what seems like miles and looks like inches on her map. Claire suspects they have been making pointless detours, but she doesn't care. She likes looking at the river as it slides past, secret in its own business but keeping an eye on them. She likes the bustle of Oxford Circus, the aimless people-watching of Piccadilly and the purposeful stride along Saville Road.

They have peered in shop windows at jewellery and buttons. They have poured tea from dribblesome teapots and drunk from flowery china cups. They have bitten into crisp apples sold off a barrow, and tried on hats and ladies' gloves. They have browsed through shelves of second-hand books and managed to leave empty-handed. They have fed the ducks in St James' Park and tried to walk through all the green bits they can find. There are a lot of them and their legs are tired.

'I think it's that way.' Jennifer points the direction they've just come.

'Are you sure?' Claire asks, getting to her feet.

'Nope, but it's roughly that way.'

Jennifer shoves the map back into her pocket and slips her arm through her mother's, smiling happily.

'Besides, we're having fun, aren't we?'

Claire laughs, 'Yes, we are. It's lovely spending the day together. Even if you are completely insane.'

'Must run in the family.' Jennifer gives her arm a squeeze. They walk companionably down Pall Mall, each lost in thought.

'What are you thinking?' Claire asks.

'Funny isn't it, how that tube map is so straight and neat, making everything look planned when really it's all a big mess?'

'Well, they couldn't exactly lay it out how it is, could they?'

'Why not? Other maps are, you know, road maps and that. I suppose I knew it wasn't to scale, but I really did think it was more accurate than it was. Imagine if that really was all you had to navigate by, you'd get completely lost! And it calls itself a map. You could sue under the trade descriptions act or something.'

Claire laughs. 'Well, you could. But I don't think you'd get very far. It's a representation isn't it? And when you're underground, you can't see where you're going, so it doesn't really matter does it? All that counts is the destination. And it's very detailed, so you know which interchanges to use and when to switch lines. I always thought it was an amazing design.'

'I'm not saying it isn't, but... I don't know. It seems slightly deceptive somehow! I mean, it all looks so ordered underneath, but it's nothing like that on the surface.'

They turn into St James' Square and they fall off the map, strolling through London arm-in-arm in no man's land. When they arrive at Burlington Arcade and the Royal Academy, they stand still at the bottom of the steps, transfixed by the banner. It reads "Journeys: a collection by Adam Burns". Afraid to move, they clutch each other, all thoughts of convenient design are gone.

'This is our destination' whispers Claire and they climb the steps to the gallery.

****

'It's just all so deep isn't it? I wish I could fall into it.'

The woman tilts her head so the blonde hair falls back over her shoulder and the man beside her nods appreciatively. He leans forward until his nose is inches away from the canvas and utters a bark of a laugh, which the woman echoes and they nod again and move smiling to the next painting, continuing their strange staccato exchange of ejaculations and interjections.

'I wish you could too' Jennifer mutters under her breath.

She holds the empty glass tightly in her hand, knowing she shouldn't get another one yet. This evening will be long and she wants to be able to congratulate Adam and mean it. She surreptitiously polishes the glass on her skirt, but she can't wipe away the smudged thumbprints and she feels terribly uncouth. She glances at her watch. She is rationing herself to no more than a glass of champagne every half hour and there are still another twenty minutes to go.

Sighing, she takes another look at the picture on the wall. It is a deep blue with swirls of green and orange. She tries to look contemplative and intelligent. Perhaps it is an ocean crossed by vibrantly coloured container ships – that could be possible couldn't it? She read somewhere that quite a lot of containers go missing, simply fall overboard and get washed up on island shores. She doesn't remember the exact statistic – her father would be horrified – but she remembers being surprised at the number. She smiles to think of a load of islanders tripping around in Wonder Woman boots.

'Concentrate', she tells herself sharply and tries to affect the tilted head position from the woman before. Out of the corner of her eye she tries to see if anyone is looking at her and spotting her for a fraud. She hopes no one comes and talks to her attempting to engage her in arty conversation. Nope, no one is looking and they all seem to be having highly erudite critical conversation of their own, although they all seem complimentary from the snatches she overhears.

The music is quite loud – they're playing The Jam, which she is sure is Adam's choice. At least that's one thing she understands and she taps the glass in time.

Okay, so maybe it's a DNA Helix, although she's pretty sure they intersect a little bit more than that, and they have things in the middle like a rope-ladder that hangs out of a helicopter and twists randomly in the wind, except it isn't random at all apparently.

Perhaps it's a blue chopping board and those are curls of apple and orange peel, for some homely baked pie or exotic cocktail. Or perhaps not. Right, another fifteen minutes. She moves to the next painting. Maybe they've hung it upside down by mistake?

'What's it supposed to be?'

Jennifer turns with relief to see Emma who thrusts a full glass at her and shrugs out of her jacket while trying to drink her own.

'I'm not exactly sure, but apparently you can lose yourself in it.'

Emma raises one eyebrow at her – a talent Jennifer has always envied.

'If you say so. I love our brother and I'm sure it's all very good and everything, but I don't understand the first thing about art, and I'm sure half of these pretentious hangers-on don't either.'

They scan the warm room full of murmuring and chattering and appreciating and they laugh. Jennifer feels the tension drain from her. Emma always knows how to handle these situations and she never minds admitting her ignorance about anything; neither of them have ever been to a gallery opening before.

'Right, I'm going to get rid of this coat, get us another glass and then we can find a quiet spot and have a chat. I just found out the speeches are in about an hour, so Adam will be being fawned over until then. Where's mum?'

'I think she's with Adam.'

'Excellent. That'll keep her happy playing the proud parent. Ruth phoned me before to say she'd be late, and Dad's coming straight from work, so there's no one else worth talking to.'

'Thanks a lot!'

'Yeah well, it's not often I get a night off.'

Emma has managed to deposit her coat, get another two glasses of champagne and find a place to sit, just as she said she would, all in the time while she has been talking. Jennifer follows her like a lamb. She wonders whether this is what makes Emma so good at her job. The animals must just trust her direct simplicity, knowing she is doing the best for them that she can, without getting carried away on a tide of emotion. Has she always been like this? Bossing her little sister about? Is that why Jennifer is always told that she's very good at taking direction? Funny how things work out.

'What are you smiling at? You're getting as potty as the rest of them.'

****

Claire takes off her rings and rubs moisturiser into her hands. The skin is slightly wrinkled and losing its elasticity. She pinches it and watches it slowly fall back into place. It seems to take longer each day, but she doesn't really mind. She doesn't think it is that important.

She looks in the mirror and sees James infinitely reflected back in the angled frame. He is sitting up in bed in their hotel room, watching her with his hands clasped behind his head. Suddenly she blushes and feels ridiculously shy.

'Are you looking at me?'

'Yes.' He doesn't take his eyes off her and she turns to face him, slightly unnerved by his myriad image. She smiles at his singular version.

'Why?'

'You're my beautiful wife. Can I not look at my beautiful wife?'

She laughs, but she is pleased. She has had a wonderful night. It was great to see Adam and the girls. They are all doing so well. Sometimes she is amazed to think she had a hand in creating them. James seems to read her thoughts.

'We did alright, didn't we?'

Claire stands and crosses the room to sit beside him on the bed.

'I worry about them all still. I know they're adults and making their own way in the world, but it just seems to get so hard.'

'It is hard, but we raised them well. They can cope with it. And they always know they have us to help if we can.'

Claire nods and strokes his hand absently. There are tears in the corners of her eyes and she doesn't know why. Sometimes she feels this emotion welling up from nowhere and she doesn't know what to do with it, so it seems to leak out of her. James pulls her close and kisses the top of her head. He just holds her gently until she feels calm and safe. He kisses her again and holds her at arm's length.

'Right, now we're in a hotel room in the middle of London on a wild weekend. And you want to talk about the children?'

He raises a lascivious eyebrow and she laughs and allows herself to be pulled onto the bed.

3

Knightsbridge

Zone 1: Piccadilly (between South Kensington and Hyde Park Corner).

Nearby attractions: Apsley House; Harrods; Royal Albert Hall.

Knightsbridge is the only tube station on the London Underground network to have six consecutive consonants in its name.

The underground route between Knightsbridge and South Kensington is particularly tortuous as it twists and turns to avoid a plague pit, where victims of the Black Death were buried.

Originally a small village outside the City of London, Knightsbridge has become the location of some of the most prestigious retail outlets (Harrods; Harvey Nichols; Liberty) and home to some of the world's richest people.

Apsley House was originally the London residence of the first Duke of Wellington, and was known as Number One, London, being the first house past the Knightsbridge toll gate. The Wellington family maintain rooms there, making it the only property managed by the English Heritage in which the original owners' family still live. It is open to the public who can admire the Duke's formidable collection of paintings, porcelain and silver.

From a simple fruit and vegetable shop with two assistants and a messenger boy, Harrods has grown to be the biggest department store in Europe. In early December 1883 it burnt to the ground, while still making all its Christmas deliveries and making record profits. In 1898 it introduced England's first 'moving staircase' and offered brandy to nervous passengers to help them cope with the escalating terror. In 1989 it introduced a dress code.

****

Claire smiles as she listens to the radio. She likes the comedy programmes and the quizzes. She laughs occasionally as she fills in the pastry cases with mincemeat. She is happy. She knows the children will laugh at her for going to all this trouble, but it is Christmas and she wants to make a big deal over it. She loves having her family around her and she expresses her love through food. When they mock her she reminds them that she lived through a war. There was a time when you weren't sure where your next meal was coming from. Now she can feed them the traditional yuletide meal; turkey with cranberry sauce, even though no one likes it, and home-made stuffing.

She looks forward to seeing her grandchildren. Emma's girls are delightful, and they make her feel younger. They love their life in Yorkshire where Emma runs her own practice with her husband, Phil. Adam's wife, Patricia, has just had her second baby and was worried that it would be too much with them all in the house together, but Claire has persuaded her to come down from Wales. Ruth is coming up from Brighton where she has been working on her latest collection. Claire can't wait for the house to be full of laughter and little children running around again.

She has lots to do and she enjoys being busy. She glances at her list taped to the fridge and is satisfied to see several things crossed off. She will make the beds up when the mince pies are in the oven, and clear out the back bedroom so the girls will have somewhere to sleep. She did it not long ago and can't imagine where all the boxes come from. They must breed or something. Surely she doesn't accumulate all this stuff!

James is upstairs on a ladder, painting the windows. It is an endless job, and he has to start again the minute he has finished to stop the gloss from peeling and the damp from getting in. He quite likes it. It is monotonous and he doesn't have to think. The football news rattles on in the background. James is anxious to hear about Arsenal; to check that everyone is fit who should be. He wonders whether Adam will be at one of the grounds taking photos and he listens to where Spurs are playing. He knows that Adam only supports Spurs because they are Arsenal's rivals and though this used to bother him, they have become more amicable about it all these days and now they enjoy the banter.

When he hears the announcement on the news, he turns ashen and lays down his brush. He clings onto the ladder and slowly descends the rungs. He doesn't believe in God, but he prays silently.

'Please, no. Not now. She couldn't cope.'

He walks into the kitchen and Claire is still chuckling at *I'm Sorry, I Haven't a Clue*. She smiles at him and puts the kettle on. He sits and waits for the phone to ring with good news. He has never been good at hiding his feelings.

'Is everything alright, darling?' she asks him.

He guides her to a chair and places a cup of tea in front of her.

'I'm sure there's no need to worry, but they've just said on the news that there's been an explosion in Knightsbridge.'

Her hand flies to her mouth and her eyes open wide.

'Jennifer!'

Jennifer is in London, performing in a musical on the West End. She is "just in the chorus" she says, but she is pleased with herself. They have a Christmas break and she told them she was going shopping today before the matinee and that she will travel down tomorrow. James nods and tries to think of something reassuring.

'There's no news of casualties. The police are there. I'm sure she'll be fine. We would have heard something.'

Claire gets up and goes through to the living room. She turns on the television and sinks into a chair. The news comes on with pictures of a plume of smoke over Harrods. There are sirens and loud speakers. People are asked to clear the area. There is blood and glass and so many people with dark green shopping bags, running and screaming; some are standing looking bewildered. Police cordon off the streets with white plastic tape and dogs seem to be sniffing for something.

The news reporters know nothing. There are injuries, and eyewitnesses talk of glass flying everywhere and rubble and noise. They are baffled, defiant, angry, scared. They are persistently asked to clear the area. There are reports of another unexploded device. There is panic and chaos.

James hovers in the doorway. He can't stand and he can't sit. He turns off the television, but Claire remains staring at the screen. She is trying not to think about the war-time blast when they were children, when she looked after Jean and searched for her mother, and she feels the same empty feeling as then.

It seems like hours before the phone rings. They both jump up and Claire runs to snatch it up. She drops it in her haste and fumbles with the receiver.

'Mum, it's me. I don't know if you've seen anything, but...'

'Jennifer!'

Claire looks to James and nods frantically. He sighs and releases the breath he has been holding all afternoon.

'My God, are you okay?'

'I'm okay Mum. I thought I should call you, but I'll have to go now. There's a massive queue for the phone and we're being moved on. I'll be alright, don't worry. I'll be home tomorrow.'

'Are you sure you're alright? What happened? Where are you?'

'Yes, I'm fine. It was close though. I was... I saw people everywhere, it was just awful... I've lost my shopping. I don't know what I'm going to do about presents now.'

Claire sinks to the floor. She grips the receiver and her knuckles are white.

'You could have been killed,' she whispers.

'Look, Mum, I'm fine. I'll come home as soon as I can. They're clearing the streets and I've got to move on now.

But I'll get home somehow. Don't worry about me, Mum. I'll see you soon. I love you, but I've got to go. Okay?'

Claire nods silently but she doesn't realise her daughter can't see her.

'Okay, Mum?'

'Yes, yes, everything will be okay. Take care. Look after yourself. Come home.'

She stays on the floor listening to the purring of the dial tone. 'I love you too.'

James crouches beside her and takes the phone from her hands like a child, placing it gently back in the cradle. He sits on the floor and puts his arm around her, holding her tightly as she rocks and cries tears of sorrow and relief.

'She's okay. She's alive. Thank God.'

James bites back the words he has to say about God. There is a bomb in the middle of the capital on one of the busiest shopping days of the year, just over a week before Christmas. The police suspect the IRA – they claim to fight on religious beliefs. That's the God she's thanking. But if their daughter is safe and if his wife doesn't have to suffer another loss just now then she can thank whomever she wants. He waits for her shoulders to stop shaking and gives them a squeeze.

'Drink?'

4

Ealing Common

Zone 3: District (between Ealing Broadway and Acton Town), Victoria (between North Ealing and Acton Town).

Nearby attractions: Ealing Common; Ealing Studios; Pitzhanger Manor Gallery and House.

Ealing Common was designated common land by the 1866 Metropolitan Commons Act. The large open space of almost 50 acres is planted with horse chestnut trees (most of which come from the late Victorian period) and London plane trees with a large English oak tree in the centre. It was designed by Charles Jones, an architect, engineer and surveyor who was also responsible for designing town halls, schools, churches, libraries and the local fire engine station. He laid out Ealing's first proper sewage system, designing a sewage farm to treat the effluent from the Thames. When charged with designing the first Electricity Generating Station and distribution system, he designed a filter for the sludge from the sewage farm next-door to be burnt as fuel to provide power.

The nearby Ealing Studios is the oldest continually working film studio in the world. Built for the use of sound in early British films, the studio produced many films in the 30s and 40s starring the likes of George Formby and Will Hay.

Mornington Crescent

After the war the company focussed on the Ealing comedies, many of which have become classics of British cinema.

****

The cat winds around Claire's legs, nearly making her trip over as she carries her groceries in from the car. She stumbles and stops herself from swearing at it. It's not the cat's fault. She loves the cat.

'Oh Horatio, get out of it!'

She puts down the plastic bags and picks up the black and white creature who headbutts her with delight. She stokes him under the chin and listens to him purr, as he flattens his ears and closes his eyes, stretching out his neck in supplication.

If she's honest she would have to admit she got him when the children left home. It wasn't as if she needed another child, but she cuddles him with maternal fervour. He seems to enjoy it and is always waiting for her on the doorstep when she comes home. How can she fail to be moved?

He pours his furry body back to the linoleum and pads around the bags.

'Alright, hold your horses!' Claire laughs at the inappropriate image, picturing a cat in charge of a carriage and four. She drifts gently into a Cinderella reverie – wasn't the footman a cat in that?

She rummages through the bags and finds the tinned cat food. She has gone up-market from the usual jelly meat. It is an indulgence, she knows, but one she can afford. With no children to feed, no mortgage left to pay and a steady income, she is determined that she can buy whatever she wants.

Sometimes she longs for the day she can retire. She is already tired. She examines the similarity of the words in her head. Why don't they call it reawakenment? She would like to wake again – to do the things she's never done. What would she do, she wonders, given the time? She would sleep first of all, to catch up on all the hours stolen from her by work.

She no longer really enjoys teaching. It's all paperwork and dull forms rather than bright minds. She spends more time in meetings with staff than in her class with children. She no longer feels that she inspires them. She just stops them fighting with each other and taking drugs. And the parents come to the school and threaten the teachers who dare to breathe the word discipline.

She shudders at the thought of last week's parent's meeting when a father told her that his son didn't need O-levels as he would get him a job at the BBC regardless. How could you compete with that? She wishes she could ask for him to be removed from class if he doesn't want to learn, but they have a duty to keep him there, scowling and disruptive, nodding along to his Walkman. Her class has become a crèche for big babies and indolent parents to offload their offspring. It wasn't meant to be like this.

Claire takes out her receipt and sits at the table, ticking off the items before she puts them away. She doesn't really know why she does this, as she's hardly going to get back into the car and drive back to the supermarket if something's missing or she's been overcharged. She supposes it is just part of her routine and she likes routine. She restocks the fruit bowl and the chest freezer – there are things in there that she can't remember existing. One day she knows she will have to defrost and clear it out, but the thought depresses her slightly. Surely that isn't what she will be doing in her retirement?

The tins are lined up in the pantry, facing forwards and she throws away the old mould encrusted cheeses and replaces them with fresh. She snips opens packets and cartons and decants them into click clack boxes and plastic containers. The toiletries are taken upstairs and distributed around the bathroom and the medicine cabinet. James thinks these things – toilet rolls; soaps; toothbrushes and headache tablets – come from the pharmacy fairy.

She leaves the flowers until last. These are her favourite aspect of shopping. She has a collection of vases which she fills with carnations and freesias, snipping of the ends and displaying the scents and colours on mantelpieces, windowsills and on top of the piano. She avoids lilies. She has read they are poisonous to cats, although James says this is scaremongering and the cat will avoid anything that is dangerous. Maybe he will; maybe he won't – why take chances?

As she carries a vase of pink and white carnations to the telephone table, Claire glances at the doormat where a smattering of letters lies in the hallway. She always comes in through the side door – the tradesman's entrance – and the postman arrives after they have both left for work so she never sees the post until the afternoon.

She scans an expert eye over the envelopes – nothing handwritten. No news today of her children scattered through the country with their various lives, jobs and relationships. Sometimes they send postcards; occasionally they write letters. Jennifer writes a lot – random missives about books and plays; Ruth is more of an efficient phone caller. Adam finds cards of artworks that interest him and Emma sends photos of the children. Claire pins them all up on the kitchen wall. James says it looks a mess but she likes it – she thinks of it as a metaphor for family life. He just rolled his eyes when she told him this, but he stopped complaining about the chaotic collage.

Picking up the confetti correspondence she sifts idly through the bills and puts them to one side. James deals with them. It is one of the many things in their relationship that is divided into gender stereotypes. She does the shopping and the cooking; he pays the bills and mows the lawn. He always drives when they go away for weekends unless he has a drink and then he sits critically in the passenger seat tut-tutting at her cautious roundabout technique which puts her on edge until he falls asleep and lolls his head against the window.

There's the free local press that comes each weekend. She'll read that later although there will be nothing of interest. Shocking street furniture vandalism and raffles for a new scout hut or a rowing regatta and some parent bragging about their child's musical achievements. The pictures from the local football club always make her laugh. She empathises with the solitary fans looking nonplussed on the sidelines while the photographer attempts to capture an image of someone covered in mud doing something mildly skilful with a football, rather than just flailing wildly in midair.

One envelope is heavier than the others and the address is printed in a bold, assured font. Claire's mouth goes dry although there is no reason for it. She checks that it really is their address and not some mistake – it is addressed just to her – Mrs C. Burns. It looks official and she wonders who can have sent it?

Horatio looks up at her with big green eyes and she laughs aloud.

'I'll only know by opening it, won't I?'

She tears open the cream envelope and sits down at the kitchen table to read the embossed letter within. She reads it again and swears softly.

'Bloody hell.'

****

Claire is startled from her reverie by the signature rap on the front door that James always gives when he gets home – no tradesman's entrance for him. Claire lets him in and he gives her a kiss before striding into the hallway and dropping his briefcase on the floor. He heads to the kitchen but pauses. Everything is in darkness and there are no familiar cooking smells. Only then does he realise that Claire is slightly shell-shocked.

'Is everything alright?'

'I got a letter.'

He waits for further explanation but none is forthcoming, so he circles his hand impatiently,

'And?'

She passes him the envelope and he scans it quickly, taking in names and numbers. He looks at her and mutters, 'Who? Wha...?'

'Aunty Beatrice' she whispers, almost inaudibly. 'But I don't know why. We were never what you'd call close. Dad's sister, remember? She came to Mum's funeral and I was surprised to see her there. We made up for our past differences, but I haven't heard from her since. I would never have thought...'

Claire trails off as James turns on the light and reads the letter again, slowly this time. When he has finished he whistles softly.

'Ten thousand quid! You never told me she was rich.'

'I didn't know. I don't know. Like I said, I haven't heard anything from her since Mum's funeral. She never approved of my mother and she didn't want Dad to marry her in the first place. Then there was that business at Dad's funeral... I mean, we sort of cleared that up, but we didn't become great friends or anything. She was never that sort of aunt. I can't imagine why she would leave this to me. I've been thinking all day it must be some mistake, but it's all so official. So final. Why would she...?'

'Old age does strange things to people. Maybe she had no other family. How old was she?'

Claire shrugged, remembering the beetle of a woman who had always seemed ancient to her. 'I suppose she would have been about ninety.'

'Well, I'll make us a cup of tea and you can tell me what you're going to do with it.' James fills the kettle and switches it on, taking mugs from the cupboard and swirling warm water around the teapot. Claire remembers her father's funeral and how Aunty Beatrice checked the cups for dust. And then her mother's funeral with the uneaten sandwiches and the broken teapot. There seems to be far too much tea in her history and it all seems to be connected with death.

'Can't we have something stronger?'

5

Kew Gardens

Zone 3: District (between Gunnersbury and Richmond).

Nearby attractions: Hampton Court Palace; Kew Bridge Steam Museum; The National Archives; The Royal Botanic Gardens at Kew.

Kew Gardens Tube Station has a number of distinguishing features: the Victorian station buildings are protected as part of the Kew Gardens conservation area; the footbridge over the tracks is Grade II listed (applied to 'particularly important buildings of more than special interest'); and it is the only station on the London Underground network with a pub attached to it – originally named 'The Railway'.

The Royal Botanic Gardens at Kew (more usually called Kew Gardens) contains the world's largest collection of living plants. Some of the plant life in captivity at Kew is extinct in the wild. The gardens contain both the world's largest Victorian glasshouse (the Temperate House) and Britain's smallest royal palace (Kew Palace).

The close-at-hand Hampton Court Palace is on a far larger scale and was Henry VIII's favourite palace (he had over 60). The palace had tennis courts, bowling alleys, pleasure gardens, a hunting park (of more than 1,000 acres), massive kitchens, a fine chapel, a vast communal dining room and a multiple 'garderobe' (toilet) that could seat 28 people at a time, known as The Great House of Easement.

****

'They all said I should do whatever *I* want with it.'

Claire realises that she sounds petulant and defensive, but this is what her children had said when she asked them what they thought she should do with the money. She sits opposite Valerie who is playing mother, pouring more tea from the flowery teapot, concentrating on not spilling any of the precious brown liquid. It is expensive here, which is one of the reasons they like it.

Now that Claire has retired she meets Valerie for afternoon tea once a month at this old stately house. There is a chill in the air so they sit in the conservatory, but they can see the broad sweep of the river, and the green and grey colours shot through with brilliant reds and yellows settle softly like a tapestry in the background of their conversation.

'Well, yes, but is that really what you want to do? You could invest it, or use it as a deposit on a cottage or something, so you have somewhere to get away from it all.'

'But I don't want to get away from it all. I actually quite like it all. We've lived here for so long and there are so many memories, that I don't know that I'd want to start again somewhere else. I know it sounds silly, but I like to think there is somewhere familiar for the children to come back to whenever they want.'

'Hmm, but it seems so…' Valerie casts about for the word as she reaches for another club sandwich.

Mornington Crescent

'Frivolous?' Claire suggests, and laughs as she adds milk to her teacup and stirs rather more ferociously than she had planned.

'But that's what I want. I feel as though I've always done things for others and everything has been planned. Career; relationships; saving money for the children... And now they're all grown up and doing alright, and my career is over and I could invest it, but I hardly think this is the right time.'

Valerie looks chastened. Her daughter's husband has been stung by the recent stock market crash, and she has spent the last half an hour at least talking about it. They may lose the house and their lifestyle of pony clubs in the leafy suburbs. Sometimes it is hard to hear of your friend's good fortune when you are worrying about your children's lack of it.

'Besides, I may not be around for that long, and I want to enjoy myself while I can. Life's short enough as it is, and it can be even shorter for some.'

Her eyes fill with tears as she thinks of her sister. Valerie is used to these sentimental reminisces and she reaches out to her friend's hand and squeezes it gently.

'I know love, I know. Here, have one of these little fairy cakes.'

With their pink icing and silver cachous the tiny treats look as though they might fly off the third tier of the cake stand and Claire takes one gratefully. Valerie selects a square of chocolate fudge and rolls it around in her mouth in silence.

'But why New Zealand?' she asks at last.

Claire smiles and shrugs, 'Why not?'

Valerie looks nonplussed – flippant is not a word she would usually use to describe Claire.

'I mean, I looked at all the brochures and it looks like an amazing place. They've got mountains, volcanoes, beaches, forests, glaciers, boiling mud, you name it; it's all there in one easy-to-get-around country. And they speak the same language – apart from that accent – so I won't have a language barrier. People say it's like here in a simpler bygone time. I'm quite looking forward to that.'

Valerie still looks unconvinced, although she is thawing.

'If you say so. If it were me, I'd choose Spain or the Canary Islands – somewhere hot where I could lie on a beach, sipping sangria and getting a suntan.'

'I know, and I thought about that, briefly. But I don't want to lie around; I want to see things and do things. I want to experience nature in all its glory before it all gets built up and disappears. And James would hate to lie on a beach.'

Valerie nods as she reaches for a slice of Battenberg cake. She breaks the pink and yellow cake into separate squares, which she always does and which Claire always finds mildly annoying. Why would they bother to put them together with apricot jam, if all you are going to do is break them apart?

'So, it's all about him really?'

'No!' Claire is frustrated – she doesn't seem to be getting through. She tries again.

'The world is such a big place and there is so much to see. I've hardly ever seen any of it. I've been busy working and raising children... Don't get me wrong, I don't regret it for a second. But my sister travelled and she always made it sound so exciting – discovering new things – and I've got the opportunity to do so now.'

She absently plops a blob of clotted cream onto a light fluffy scone as she continues,

'And my mum, you know, she always wanted to go there. We didn't even know that, but she told us one day when Jean and I went to visit. We were really surprised, because she's never said anything before. And I thought, how sad, that you could have a dream but keep it to yourself because you never thought it would come true.

'You see, I've got the chance to make her dream come true in a way. And the weird thing is, it came from out of the blue. I wasn't expecting it at all. Aunty Beatrice has been the last person on my mind, but she must have thought of us, to leave me so much money in her will. I think she would have split it between us if Jean had still been alive. So it's sort of hers too. I feel like I'm keeping a promise, although I never made one. It's like they'll both be with me when I go.'

Valerie dabs at the corners of her mouth with the linen napkin and she holds her hands up, smiling in mock surrender.

'Okay, okay, New Zealand it is then!'

As they walk arm in arm around the gardens they admire the impeccably planted flowerbeds. Splashes of pink dahlias mingle with singing orange asters. Claire knows the names of the garden plants and flowers, and the birds that flit among the trees or swoop along the river.

She used to tell them to her mother and now she offers them to Valerie in a bouquet of knowledge. Valerie loves the colourful blooms but she asks the same questions week after week. Claire suspects she doesn't listen to the answers, but she doesn't mind supplying them over and over again.

Valerie admires the glowing showy autumn flowers that last through the colder months. Claire prefers the hardy dandelions whose strength belies their delicate appearance. She likes the flowers best when they have gone to seed, bending and shaking their white locks in the wind; gifting their future life to the fertile earth before going to sleep for the winter.

Their shoes crunch on the gravel as they walk off their meal. They pause on the overhanging balcony to watch a heron picking its way along the riverbank, occasionally stabbing its beak into the water and gobbling down a fish. It looks faintly ridiculous with its long skinny legs and infinitesimal movements, reminding Claire of an old lady in a raincoat, surrounded by faded hauteur and the memory of glamour. When they hear its mournful call boom across the valley, she is struck even more by the likeness.

The heron decides it has had enough of this fishing spot. It begins to pedal its feet and flap its wings, finally taking to the air with its neck tucked back to its body and its legs trailing down behind. It looks ungainly as it heads off on its adventures and Claire smiles. Thinking of her previous comparison, she wonders if it is an avian embodiment of her prospective travels. She doesn't voice this thought aloud. Valerie thinks she is crazy enough as it is.

They return to their cars, which are the only ones left in the car park. Dusk is falling and they will go home to their brightly lit houses and think about housework or the evening meal. Perhaps they will watch the news and see the international disasters brought to the corner of their front room. They both linger, not wanting to break this ethereal moment.

'So when do you go?'

'We leave on Tuesday morning. It takes ages to get there. I don't think we actually arrive until Thursday.'

'You'll send me a postcard?'

'Of course.' The women embrace in the failing light and turn to leave. Almost as an afterthought, Valerie calls from the car,

'Have fun!'

Claire smiles and waves, 'I fully intend to.'

6

Mornington Crescent

Zone 2: Northern (between Camden Town and Euston).

Nearby attractions: Camley Street Natural Park; Jewish Museum; Royal Veterinary College.

In 1992 the station of Mornington Crescent in Camden Town was closed down to repair the 85-year-old lifts. The idea was that it would reopen within the year, but the station was found to be in a state of disrepair needing much work and there was talk of closing it permanently.

A campaign was launched to reopen the station due its popularity on account of the BBC Radio 4 panel game in I'm Sorry I Haven't a Clue. The station was reopened in 1998 by the regular cast of the show.

Camley Street Natural Park is a small but thriving wild green space on the banks of the Regent's Canal. Created from an old coal yard in 1984, the site is run by the London Wildlife Trust whose intention is to encourage and support wildlife in urban spaces. The ponds, wetlands, meadows and woodlands provide a natural habitat for birds, butterflies, amphibians and plants.

****

Mornington Crescent

Claire sits on the tube and watches the darkness outside. Sometimes it is illuminated by beacons for impossible dreams. The tiles are pasted over with temptations which can make you perfect if you have the money. They seem to announce that you can buy beauty, thinness and happiness – these things are interchangeable in subterranean advertisements.

Sometimes she sees her reflection. She is old, but the thought doesn't bother her. She may not have flawless skin, gleaming teeth, an espresso maker (why have one in your home when half of the fun is going out to the café in the first place?) or one of those things you plug into that look like an IV drip, slowly infiltrating your conscience with media medication.

But she has good friends, a healthy family and a husband who loves her. It might not amount to much in the grand scheme of things, but she can live with that. She smiles as other people's lives flash past. She wonders what they do and why the grumpy ones look sad. She wants to tell them to focus on the positive, but she knows she will just sound like a nutter. She laughs, and from the look she receives from the young girl opposite, it is too late. She almost laughs again, but she stifles it in a fake yawn. That appears to be far more acceptable on the Northern line.

She hugs her bag to her chest. It contains her latest travel tickets. Ever since that trip to New Zealand all those years ago, she has travelled every year to all sorts of destinations. She has seen temples in Thailand, giraffes in Kenya and cricket in Barbados. She sent postcards and kept journals of each trip, into which she pasted pictures and brochures; images and memories.

When Jennifer saw one, she insisted on sending it away to a travel magazine. Claire was amazed when it was published – she had never thought of herself as a writer. Now the magazine pays her to travel and report back. She thinks of the readership as elderly middle-class housewives who somehow haven't plucked up the courage to do it themselves yet. She hopes that they do, and if there is no longer any need for her reports, she will be happy. Today she has been at the magazine offices, and they seem pleased with her and what she's doing. She basked in their approval. Now she is on her way home, but there's no hurry and she finds she enjoys even this little journey. She can stop off wherever she wants and explore any new little park or avenue that takes her fancy. It's a freedom she finds utterly delicious – a release from the tyranny of time constraints.

She has become quite the celebrity, although she uses a pseudonym and will not allow her photo to be published, wishing to remain anonymous. She is so used to defining herself as someone in relation to someone else she has quite forgotten how to be herself. Is she her mother's daughter, her sister's sister, her children's mother, her husband's wife, her niece's aunt, her pupils' teacher, or simply Claire?

She is mystified by the cult of fame and the things people will do on television to get their five seconds-worth; what store must the general public set by eating live insects or flashing their knickers? It is this miscomprehension rather than her wrinkled face, grey hair and spectacles that make her feel her age.

James is bemused by it all. He says she must have inherited it from her mother – she doesn't know if he means the writing or the wanderlust. Joyce did all her travelling in her mind, and Claire feels her company whenever she takes to the skies. She leaves James behind and he meets her at the airport when she returns, keen to hear her adventures.

His time is consumed by reading of the latest scientific discoveries and keeping up with complicated mathematics. Computers are a boon for him and he doesn't want to miss a thing. Claire is surprised to find that she enjoys travelling alone, but she also loves to return home to his loving arms and a deep warm bath.

She eagerly anticipates the next trip, which is one she has paid for herself with her earnings. She is going to see Dawn in California, where she lectures in anthropology at Stanford University. It will be good to see her again; it's been too long. She will be there for Thanksgiving, which she has never really celebrated before officially, although she frequently reminds herself of all the things for which she is thankful.

She will catch the greyhound bus to Pine Ridge where she is going to stay on a ranch and learn how to ride a horse. At least; she hopes she is going to learn to ride a horse. When she placed the booking, the people tried, and failed, to hide their surprise. It seems they don't get many 75 year old women wanting to learn to ride. They told her not to expect great things. But she does. Expect great things; it's her new motto.

As the tube pulls into the station, Claire opens her eyes. She sees the roundel on the wall – Mornington Crescent. She remembers listening to the game on the radio, all those years ago in another lifetime. She loves how the lack of rules made anything possible. She has not intended to get off here, but why not? There is nothing and no one she must answer to, and no plans she must keep.

Claire alights on the platform and plunges into the crowd, allowing herself to be swept along in whatever direction. She exits the station and turns left.

Printed in December 2022
by Rotomail Italia S.p.A., Vignate (MI) - Italy